NORWEGIAN FIRE

Recent Titles by Julian Jay Savarin from Severn House

HORSEMEN IN THE SHADOWS
MACALLISTER'S RUN
PALE FLYER
STRIKE EAGLE
TARGET DOWN
TYPHOON STRIKE

NORWEGIAN FIRE

Julian Jay Savarin

SEVERN SH HOUSE

This first hardcover edition published in Great Britain 1998 by
SEVERN HOUSE PUBLISHERS LTD of
9–15 High Street, Sutton, Surrey SM1 1DF.

British Library Cataloguing in Publication Data

Savarin,   Julian Jay
            Norwegian fire. – (Wings ; 5)
            1.   Great Britain. Royal Air Force - Fiction
            2.   World War, 1939-1945 - Aerial operations, British - Fiction
            3.   War stories
            1.   Title
            823.9'14 [F]

            ISBN 0-7278-5391-0

Typeset by Hewer Text Ltd.,
Edinburgh, Scotland.
Printed and bound in Great Britain by
MPG Books Ltd, Bodmin, Cornwall.

1

Laerdal, Norway. May 1941
Per Ålvik lay flat against the steep slope, keeping his head below the skyline. The laboured whine of the engine of the German troop carrier, as it made its way up the winding mountain road, came distantly to him. He would have plenty of time to set his ambush, he reasoned, and to get away before they knew what hit them. The troop carrier was still some way down the mountain.

As he lay there he reflected upon how radically his life had changed from what it had been exactly a year earlier. Then, despite the war storms further south in mainland Europe and the increasing anxieties of the whole nation, he'd still been hoping to continue his career as an architect. True, he'd just been starting, but he'd had ideas with which he'd hoped to revolution- ize modern architecture, and not just in Norway.

He'd been looking forward to launching his designs internationally. Perhaps he could have been a new Frank Lloyd Wright.

Perhaps, he now thought grimly. How quickly dreams foundered against the rough seas of reality.

He'd been fooling himself. Nazi Germany had been crushing entire countries beneath its heel. It had only been a matter of time before it would be Norway's turn. Despite all the conciliatory propaganda about wanting to trade with a neutral Norway, the enemy had been preparing for invasion. But still he'd hung on to his dream of creating beautiful buildings; constructions for a benign civilization.

Instead, the barbarians had not only arrived at the gate but had comprehensively breached it, and were now in control. On the night of 8–9 April the year before, while everyone had still been vainly hoping that war would not come, the invasion had begun. The undermanned and under-armed national forces had not been able to cope. But the fight continued in the mountains.

The Allies should have seen it coming, he now thought. There had certainly been warning enough. We should have seen it coming. Then he raged at himself. *I* should have seen it coming.

Despite the passage of the year, he was still disgusted with the way he'd allowed his dreams to blind him. He had paid dearly for that folly; and something else had been added to the disgust. Guilt. He now carried enough to last a lifetime, although that might not prove long under the circumstances.

The Allies, with Norwegian forces, had wrested control from the enemy at Narvik, by 28 May, soundly beating him in the process. The French Foreign Legion had even captured Bjervik, thirty-two kilometres further north, in a pincer movement. All in vain. A brave, but woefully ill-prepared adventure had ended within a fortnight. The Allies, needing their troops in other theatres, had been forced to withdraw, and Norway had been left to watch the hope of a swift dispatch of the enemy comprehensively extinguished. The Germans had marched back into the battered town with its precious iron ore up for grabs, and had met no resistance. Instead, it was going to be a long, painful fight-back against the brutal invader, with no certainty of the outcome.

With the legitimate government-in-exile safely in England and the Quisling puppet serving the invaders, it was up to the members of the resistance – the Milorg and disparate underground groups – along with clandestine Allied forces, to continue the fight.

The fortunes of war had put Ålvik in command of such a group. There were just thirty in his command – including four women – but what they lacked in numbers, they more than made up for in impact. Of all the groups, they were among the most ruthless, and therefore the most feared by the enemy soldiers. They were also the most hunted.

Ålvik's transformation from dreaming creator of beautiful buildings to fearsome destroyer had begun the day he had travelled down to Bergen to visit his family, after six months in the mountains. He had taken the appalling risk because word had come that his mother had fallen dangerously ill and was not expected to live.

In the house that evening had been his father, who once had his own business and was himself not in the best of health, having been pressed into a local forced-labour group; his sixteen-year-old sister, Marianne, allowed to stay home to look after his mother; his fiancée, Elle, a teacher who now worked in a bakery; and his ten-year-old brother. And their neighbour.

Until that day Ålvik had been a reasonably courageous fighter; but there was nothing particularly special about him to distinguish him from the many other brave Norwegians who were fighting back any way they could. The events at the house, however, would eventually turn him into the sort of killer that would soon give him command of his own special team and, in turn, make him a man hunted with passion by the local SS.

The family's neighbour was a friend of many years, a man trusted by them all. What no one suspected at the time was that he was a Quisling who had been making reports about everyone who lived in the street. The arrival of Ålvik that night, smuggled into the house under the noses of the frequent patrols, was meant to have been his major coup.

A trap had been set for Ålvik's capture; but it was the young boy, Christer, who would save his older brother.

Christer had become restless and had found it difficult to come to terms with the fact that his mother was going to die. He had gone outside to sit alone, and to weep. It was then that he had seen surreptitious movement. With a wisdom beyond his years, he had given no sudden indication that he was aware of what was happening. He had remained sitting, loudly giving vent to his grief, then had gone back in as if he'd seen nothing. Once safely back in the house, he had pulled his brother to one side and whispered urgently to him.

Just then Ålvik had picked up a nervous glance in their direction, from the trusted neighbour. He had shown no reaction, but the survival instincts that had rapidly come to him during his still-limited experience in the field had made Ålvik realize instantly what was going on.

Feigning an urgent call of nature, he had sauntered out of the room as calmly as he could; but instead of making for the toilet, he had quickly headed for the cellar. There was a ground-level window down there, hidden by a high wall, and it would allow him to make his escape in the darkness. He was fortunate in that the SS troopers waiting to spring their ambush had not yet closed in on the house. He would not have made it if they had already been in place. Had it not been for Christer's impulsive rush outside . . .

Meanwhile, the boy had managed to place himself by the door to block the neighbour, in case the man should decide to follow and check if Ålvik had really gone to the toilet.

Continuing to play the picture of innocence, the neighbour had remained where he was.

However, he'd cast frequent worried glances at the door, waiting for Ålvik's return.

Ålvik had made good his escape, but his entire family and his fiancée had paid a dreadful price. His mother was shot where she lay, by the frustrated troopers who had stormed into the house. Christer was brought down by sub-machine-gun fire while trying to run. Elle and Marianne were taken away, raped repeatedly and then shot. The SS did not kill his father immediately. They made Henrik Ålvik work continuously, gradually reducing his meal rations until one day his broken heart simply gave up. He never betrayed his son.

Ålvik had then taken a searing revenge on the treacherous neighbour. He had kept well away from Bergen for several months, until the bodyguards that the terrified man had demanded from his masters were withdrawn. The underground network got the news to Ålvik that very day.

He made his last foray into Bergen one night, entered the neighbour's house and shot the man before his family, at the dinner table. He touched no one else. The man's wife, a woman who'd held Ålvik in her arms as a baby, could only stare at him with a deep sadness, shock and profound shame. She'd raised no alarm, until long after he'd gone. Ålvik had just turned twenty-one.

The local German troop commander, *Oberst* Helmut Delsingen, had himself gone to the scene. It was rumoured that he'd stared with contempt at the body, then said, 'I would have done the same.' Then he'd turned on the heels of his highly polished jackboots and walked out crisply without a backward glance or a word to the recently widowed woman.

When that story had eventually reached Ålvik, it had also carried the news that Delsingen had arrived that very night, to replace the previous commander, *Obersturmbannführer* Hans-Otto Brucht. A Waffen-SS veteran, Brucht had been put in local command of the mainly Wehrmacht, regular army, troops, to stiffen them during the initial months of the occupation. He had also brought with him a small cadre of SS officers, who were given precedence over all the Wehrmacht officers. Brucht and his SS personnel controlled the whole show.

The Wehrmacht NCOs and soldiers had not liked the idea of being under the command of an SS fanatic and his cronies, but none had possessed the courage to say so openly. The officers felt the same but they too had said nothing. They had loved ones back in

Germany who were all too vulnerable. Even at that relatively early stage of the war, they had no illusions. They had therefore followed Brucht's orders.

It had been during Brucht's term of command that the Ålvik family had met their horrific deaths. What the Milorg did not realize at the time was that Delsingen – a proper Wehrmacht officer – had been posted in because Brucht had been killed. The SS officers, however, would remain.

Brucht's staff aeroplane – a Blohm and Voss Bv138C1 – had been travelling north from Holland, where he'd been attending a high-level SS staff meeting.

Originally intended for long-range ocean recce, the Bv138 was a strange-looking beast. It was a high-wing aircraft with a flying-boat hull, and three high-mounted Junkers Jumo 205D diesels. It was slow, with a maximum speed of 171 mph. It looked like two different aeroplanes glued together, with the flying-boat hull suspended beneath the triple-engined, tail-boomed wing. It had rudimentary defensive armament. A 20mm turreted cannon was positioned ahead of the cockpit, with a similar weapon in the rear. A dorsal 13mm machine-gun was also installed behind the central engine. The Bv138 had a long range of over 2500 miles and was capable of carrying depth charges. Its service ceiling was a little over 16,000 feet; but it was in the transport role that it was most widely used, particularly in the Norwegian theatre.

Brucht had three under his command, and two of these were used in a multi-role capacity. Their hulls enabled them to be used as fast transports between the fiords, giving him the capability to quickly insert specialist teams over a wide area, to hunt out the resistance. He also used them as spotters.

The third Bv138 was reserved specifically for staff use. Brucht's aircraft was thus rigorously serviced and always in perfect operational condition. It was his great misfortune that it attracted the attentions of a pair of marauding Spitfires. The two fighters, on a daring intruder mission, had chanced upon the much slower aircraft as it had flown northwards, hugging the coastline and low over the war, clearly considering itself safe so deep within occupied airspace. The Spitfire pilots, on their way home, could hardly believe their luck when they'd come across the unescorted sitting duck.

Both aircraft had gone into the attack and within seconds the Bv138, desperately making for shallower water near the shoreline, had spiralled on to coastal rocks with explosive and fiery impact. There had been no survivors.

One of the Spitfire pilots was Johnny 'Jo-Jo' Kearns, an Australian. It would be nearly three years before the paths of Ålvik and Kearns would cross; but on that day the link that would one day bring them together had been forged.

The labouring troop carrier was rounding one of the many hairpin bends in the narrow, unmetalled mountain road. One side of the road was bordered by high earthen walls that had been hacked into the rock; the other dropped away precipitously towards the fiord far below.

Ålvik inched his head above the crest, until his eyes were exposed. He was well in cover, but he saw no reason to take chances. An alert soldier with a pair of binoculars could still spot him. He therefore ensured that his movements were infinitesimal. When he was at last satisfied with his vantage-point, he saw the half-track carrier clawing its way round another bend. It was now close enough and at its most vulnerable, as the driver became more worried about toppling off the road than about ambushes.

The rest of his body still hidden from the

enemy by the slope, Ålvik raised his left hand slowly towards the crest, then chopped it down sharply. This same action rippled through his team. When the ripple reached the last position – a mortar team – the firing began.

The hapless troop carrier, caught at the moment of negotiating the dangerous bend, came to a sudden stop as mortar shells rained down on it. Automatic fire joined the hellish noise, mercilessly raking it from nose to tail. Then came an explosion that tore great gouges out of the cliff-like border of the road as the vehicle was ripped apart. Charred, shattered bodies mingled with cascading pieces of the troop carrier as they were flung into the air and over the edge, to tumble towards the waters of the fiord. Other pieces landed in the trees or littered the ground near the burning remnants of the vehicle. Small tongues of flames, like alien creatures, licked at bits of metal and flesh. It was all over in seconds.

Swiftly but cautiously, a group of four resistance members worked their way towards the carnage, covered by their colleagues. They checked that all the troopers were dead, then laid booby-traps by the wreck before hurrying back.

As he moved down the slope to regroup with

his personnel, Ålvik did not pause to wonder about the people who had just died on his orders. Part of his mind clinically accepted that the enemy had loved ones somewhere who would mourn their passing. But he had not asked them to invade his country.

He had not asked them to do what they were doing to his own people. He had not asked them to kill his family, or to abuse and then kill the two young women who had meant so much to him. He had not asked them to destroy his dreams. He had not asked them to bring him so much grief. He would continue killing them, until every one was gone from his homeland. There was no conflict within him. As long as the war lasted he would continue to kill them, and would suffer no pangs of conscience as a result.

'The usual split,' he now said as the members of his group gathered around him. 'They'll soon come looking, but the road will be blocked for some time while they deal with our booby-traps. Watch out for the spotter planes. We'll meet at rendezvous Geiranger.'

They were going nowhere near Geiranger. It was a code for their next target. They split into smaller teams of five and headed off in different directions, into the forest and away from Laerdal.

He had spoken to them in *landsmål*, the language of the land, the tongue of the late nineteenth century, as opposed to *bokmål*, the literary language. There was a very good reason for this. Norwegian-speaking enemy agents had tried to infiltrate some of the Milorg teams. They could speak 'correct' Norwegian flawlessly. But *landsmål* trapped them every time. Even genuine Norwegians had been caught out.

Ålvik set off with the four who would be travelling with him. One was Inge Jarl.

Inge was from Tromsø, well within the Arctic Circle, and nearly two thousand kilometres from where she now was. She had *walked* from Tromsø, somehow managing to stay out of German hands during the journey. She had set off after her family had been killed in a bombing raid, not quite knowing where she was headed. She had simply wanted to get away and had eventually joined the Milorg, more by accident than by design.

On her marathon walk, she had blundered into an ambush set by a small sabotage team. A wounded German soldier, unable to move but clutching a pistol, had pointed it directly at her. She'd simply stood transfixed, staring back at him. He had died staring at her, and the pistol had fallen out of his lifeless hand.

A resistance fighter had come out of the undergrowth. 'You'd better pick that up,' he'd said to her, pointing at the pistol. 'It's yours now, and you'd better learn pretty fast how to use it.' He'd peered at her. 'I can't understand why he didn't shoot you. He must have thought you were an angel.'

That was how she'd first met Per Ålvik.

She attached herself to his team and as no one had bothered to tell her to get lost, each then seemed to have adopted the other.

Ålvik's comment about the soldier mistaking her for an angel had not been entirely grimly frivolous. Though strappingly built, her figure was richly curved. She was tall, and her very pale skin and fine blonde hair were enhanced by widely spaced, oval and slightly angled eyes of deep blue. It was a strikingly beautiful face. There was the blood of the Lapps in her veins.

When the German, a young lieutenant, had been pointing his pistol at her, the sun was at her back. Perhaps in his dying moments, the soldier had seen something no one else had. Perhaps with the sun gleaming through her golden hair, she had indeed looked like an angel to him. Whatever the reason, it had saved her life.

As Inge's stay with Ålvik's group continued to last longer than anyone expected, her performance in the field became more impressive. She learned quickly, and soon became very accurate with a mortar launcher. She was both quick and devastating. Before long, if anyone needed a good mortar on a mission they asked for Inge. On one such occasion she was wounded and nearly captured. Remembering what had happened to his sister and Elle, Ålvik had a nightmare vision of what would have happened to her.

'Her body screams for sex,' one of his men had once confided to him, waxing lyrical. 'I could just lie between those great thighs, and stay there for ever. The problem is,' he'd gone on ruefully with a sigh of deep regret, 'she's not interested. At least, not in me. She must be saving it for someone . . .' The man had looked at Ålvik. 'It's you, of course. Why don't you put the poor girl out of her misery? Probably still a virgin. You know it's you she's after.'

'Don't be ridiculous,' Ålvik had said. 'She's a child!'

'And I suppose you're an old man? More to the point, do you think you'll make it to ripe

old age? You should live that long. *We* should
live that long, at the rate we're going.'

After that scare, Ålvik had refused to let
anyone else take Inge out on further missions.
She was happy with that arrangement. Where
he went, she went.

It was Inge's mortars that had pulverized the
troop carrier. She was barely eighteen.

The commandeered building by the waterfront
was the headquarters building of Colonel
Delsingen's command.

He stood by a window looking out on the
waters of the Vågen, Bergen's inner harbour.
Directly in his line of vision were the sea-grey,
shark-like shapes of the E-boats that prowled
the fiords and frequently went out to sea to
hunt out any Tommis foolish enough to cross
the water from England to help the Norwegian
resistance. Sometimes both Norwegian and
British commandos were caught.

A knock sounded.

'*Hierein!*'

A bareheaded Wehrmacht captain came in,
and snapped to attention. He carried a sheet
of paper.

'Information on that troop carrier that set
out from Aurland, *Herr Oberst*,' he barked.

Delsingen turned slowly. A slim, athletic-looking man with close-cropped, greying hair, he had the eyes of a tolerant schoolmaster. They were eyes that had fooled many people into believing he was soft.

'How long have I been here, Geissler?'

Put slightly off balance by the unexpected question, Geissler looked uncertain, then said, 'Two months, sir.'

'Two months. In that time, what have I told you about stamping into my office and barking at me like one of those overdressed, mechanical creatures out there?'

Geissler's eyes crinkled with worry. 'Sir!' he said in a low voice. 'One of them's waiting to see you!'

'Is he? Which one?'

'*Sturmbannführer* Mindenhof, sir.' Geissler looked as if even mention of the name was a forbidden act.

Delsingen stared at him. The tolerant eyes had become less so. 'You are an officer of the Wehrmacht, man! I will not have any member of the Wehrmacht under my command being terrorized by these ... these mannequins in black. I expect you to lead by example to your men.'

'Sir ...'

18

'You are not married, are you, Geissler?'

Again the captain was momentarily caught out by this new, unexpected question. He knew the colonel would already have known that from his service file.

'No, *Herr Oberst*.' Then before he could stop himself, he added, 'I was smart.'

Delsingen studied him closely. 'Do I detect some bitterness in those words? What happened? Did she walk away?'

'I did.'

Delsingen waited.

'If the *Herr Oberst* permits, I would prefer not to talk about it.'

After a while, Delsingen said quietly, 'Very well, Geissler. We'll leave it for now. But if there is something on your mind that prevents you from giving your full attention to your duties, I expect you to tell me about it. We'll continue this later.'

'Yes, sir.'

'Now give me that message.'

Geissler handed it over.

Delsingen read it silently, then turned to look out of the window once more.

'Who found them?' he asked without turning round.

'The 138 from Aurlandsfjord spotted the

wreckage. A salvage troop is up there now. The wreck is booby-trapped.'

'He's tying us up.'

'Mountain patrols are out . . .'

'They won't find anything.'

'You said "he", sir . . . You think this is Ålvik's work?'

'I'm sure of it.' Delsingen turned to face his subordinate. 'After what was done to his family, he's carrying his own war to us. And his rage, Geissler, is of great use to the resistance movement.'

Geissler cleared his throat.

Delsingen stared at him. 'You've got something to say?'

'*Sturmbannführer* Mindenhof . . .'

'The major can wait.'

'It's Ålvik he wants to talk about, sir.'

'What you really mean, Captain, is that he believes I am not doing enough to catch these people. Presumably he wants me to take severe reprisals on the civilian population. It's this very type of reaction that has brought us this problem,' Delsingen continued in a hard voice. 'All right, Geissler. Send him in. I'm just in the mood for his nonsense.'

Geissler hesitated.

'Well?' Delsingen demanded. 'What are you waiting for?'

'Just be careful of him, sir,' Geissler advised cautiously. 'He's already managed to sneak in some SS troopers. He'll try for more.'

'Himmler's black angels don't frighten me. Send him in.'

'Yes, *Herr Oberst.*'

Geissler went out.

Seconds later, loud heels sounded outside Delsingen's door. Then it was opened by Geissler, after a discreet knock. The captain stood back for someone to enter.

Sturmbannführer Reinhardt Mindenhof, resplendent in black SS uniform, marched into the office and clicked his heels as he came to ramrod attention. Despite the control he exerted over his expression, it was clear he had not liked being made to wait.

The man seemed to gleam. His jackboots gleamed. His cross-belt gleamed. The pistol holster on his left hip, with the gun inside nestling butt forwards, gleamed. Soft, black-leather gloves were tucked into the belt, next to it. They gleamed. His cap, with its death's-head insignia, gleamed. His face gleamed. Even the very material of his back uniform seemed to gleam; and the red, white and black strip of ribbon that peeped out of his tunic drew the eye like a magnet. Iron Cross, Second Class. His hair, savagely pruned in the Himmler fashion, was a white-blond, giving the impression that he had none at all. When his cap was removed, he appeared to have a gleaming bald head. His eyes were like the night.

The dark eyes stared with evangelical fervour at the regulation portrait of Hitler that glared balefully back at him from the wall. It had been put there by Brucht. There was an even larger portrait in Mindenhof's own office.

Mindenhof was not a happy man. He was almost pathologically ambitious and, at twenty-eight, had hoped that with Brucht's death he would have received the command and the promotion that went with it. When he'd learned of his former commander's demise, he had felt an initial and very private sense of elation. In his mind, he had thanked the Tommi pilots. The command, and the promotion, were his! Now he would really show these Norwegians who was master.

But it had not turned out as he'd expected. It galled him that the decision-makers had chosen instead to send in a *full* colonel, from the *Wehrmacht*, of all things. *Two* ranks up, and still barely thirty. One more step and the man would be a general. This appointment was obviously intended to be the next stage towards general officer rank, if he did well in the post. Even worse, the Wehrmacht colonel wore the Iron Cross, *First* Class.

Ever since Delsingen had arrived, Mindenhof had been cursing the wretched Tommi pilots who had intervened so disastrously in his life. It did not occur to him to consider, even briefly, the notion that the effect on Brucht's own life had been even more disastrous – terminal, in fact.

'*Sturmbannführer* Mindenhof, *Herr Oberst!*' Geissler announced with snappy formality.

'Thank you, Geissler,' Delsingen acknowledged.

'Sir!' Geissler said as he withdrew with obvious relief, shutting the door as he did so.

Mindenhof's right arm shot out. '*Heil Hitler!*'

'What?' Oh yes. *Heil Hitler*. At ease, Major.'

Mindenhof's obsidian eyes were poisonous as he regarded his superior officer. He made no effort to disguise his disapproval of Delsingen's off-hand response to the salute.

'*Sturmbannführer!*' Mindenhof corrected him sharply, reminding the Wehrmacht officer of the preferred Waffen-SS rank.

Delsingen's eyes appeared to change in intensity as he stared back at Mindenhof.

'Don't shout, Mindenhof,' he remonstrated mildly, before going on, 'In my office, you're a major. In your office . . .'

'May I remind the colonel that as the senior Waffen-SS officer in this command . . .'

'You are my subordinate! And as far as I am aware, majors do *not* outrank colonels of *any* grade, whatever the military organization. That goes for the security police. The SS may be responsible for security in occupied areas, but here you are under *my* command. Don't you *ever* . . . interrupt me again. Is that clear, *Major*?'

For one brief and astonishing moment, Mindenhof actually quivered as he tried to control his fury. Like a gleaming black tuning fork with his feet seemingly riveted to the floor, his upper body vibrated, as if in response to a blow across the face from Delsingen.

Mindenhof, a member of the Allgemeine-SS, also belonged to the 6th SS-Totenkopfverband – one of the SS Death's-Head Units – and though these had been disbanded and amalgamated into the Waffen-SS in February that year, he and his fellow SS officers, like others in similar units, continued to swan around in their black uniforms. They liked people to know who they really were. They also relished the fact that the black outfits were very intimidating, even to other Germans. But this Wehrmacht colonel didn't seem to realize that.

'Is that clear, Major?' Delsingen repeated, stressing each word.

Mindenhof, his face pale with stifled anger, at last replied stiffly, 'Yes, sir.'

'Good. Now let's get down to business. You may remove that hat. And please take a seat.'

'I prefer to stand.' Mindenhof planted his legs apart and placed his hands behind his back. The cap stayed on. He faced Delsingen squarely, his black eyes empty.

'As you wish,' said Delsingen, who also remained standing. 'I hear you want to speak to me about the resistance fighter Ålvik.'

'The *terrorist*,' Mindenhof corrected. 'If I may be allowed to inform the *colonel*,' he continued, skirting the edges of insolence, 'when *Obersturmbannführer* Brucht was in command we had a perfect way of handling these people. The Norwegian resistance cannot properly function without help from the outside. The English send them agents, and weapons; but we have had many successes. It will not take much longer to pacify this area completely. The *Obersturmbannführer* and I –

as I have already said – did have a perfect way of attending to this.'

'I know your "perfect" way. Slaughter the civilians.'

'Their people are killing German soldiers!'

'Tell me, Mindenhof,' Delsingen began softly. 'What would you do if the Tommis – or anyone else – invaded Germany? How would you react to them?'

Mindenhof stared at him as if he had gone mad. 'That will *never* happen!'

'I am impressed by your certainty.'

'To think otherwise is not only defeatist, but unpatriotic! The Reich will prevail for . . .'

'Yes, yes. I know the rest. Happily, we do not have to worry about an invasion of the Fatherland.' Delsingen paused. The unspoken 'yet' was almost palpable. 'So let us concentrate on the problem at hand. If we were to follow the line of action you clearly favour, we would soon find ourselves receiving unwelcome attention from Berlin.'

Mindenhof stared at him.

'You don't see what I'm getting at, do you, Major?' Delsingen said.

'You are correct, Colonel. I do not.'

'Why are we here, Major?'

'You . . . *we* are here to suppress terrorist

activity while the district command secures, rebuilds and expands industry, to enable the Reich to pursue its aims. We also convert the population – who are supremely Nordic – to the German way.

'I can see you were well briefed.' Delsingen kept the irony out of his voice. 'And what do we require, to enable us to secure and expand this industry *and* convert the population?'

Again, Mindenhof looked at Delsingen as if at someone whose faculties were not quite all there. 'The area command pacifies the area. We . . . have the specific duty of hunting out the terrorists. We have specialist Wehrmacht mountain troops for this purpose. Waffen-SS mountain troops would be better, but none have been allocated to us so far. The industrial work is carried out by the defeated people, under German direction, of course . . . until they have all learned the way. Some have already done so. Quisling's Nasjonal Samlig has given us many recruits to the cause, as have the other sympathetic organizations.'

'Indeed.' Delsingen chose to ignore the pointed remark about mountain troops; and as for Quisling and the various 'sympathetic' organizations. . . 'Therefore in our specific area, we use the local populace as our labour force.'

'But naturally, Colonel.' Mindenhof was again flirting with insolence. He clearly felt Delsingen was a bit slow, and not at all equal to the important command he'd been given.

Delsingen nodded thoughtfully. 'Naturally. So how long do you think it would take for us to run out of people to supply this workforce, and to convert, if we continued with your methods? Five for every German soldier killed? Ten? Fifteen? You do not need to be a mathematical genius to realize that before long we would have no one left to do the work required – or to be converted, for that matter. What would *you* say to Berlin?'

Delsingen waited, while he secretly enjoyed watching the SS man's attempts to wriggle his way out without losing face.

'I think, Major,' Delsingen went on, before Mindenhof could say anything, 'we should call a temporary halt to the reprisals. We should concentrate on stopping the ambushes, the assassinations, the sniper attacks and the sabotage. I believe that the more victims we create, the more we feed the flames of resistance. We're giving them martyrs. If they're as ineffectual as you seem to believe, let's not give them their martyrs. Let us try another way. My way.'

'Which is?'

'I will let you have your orders in due course.'

'And, in the meantime, these attacks will continue.'

Delsingen's eyes were no longer tolerant. 'They can't sustain it for much longer. I have your word on that.'

Mindenhof clamped his jaws together. It was obvious he did not want to back down, but chose not to voice his feelings. He would fight another day.

'Very well, *Herr Oberst*,' he eventually accepted tightly. 'But if your methods do not work, I shall recommend to the High Command . . .'

'Through channels, of course. Through me, in fact.'

Mindenhof clamped his mouth shut again. His nostrils flared as he pondered his next move.

Finally he said, 'The High Command, *Waffen-SS*.' He spoke with relish. The SS High Command would sort out this upstart army man. 'May I be dismissed, Colonel?'

'You are.'

Mindenhof snapped to attention with a sharp

click of the heels. The right arm shot out. '*Heil Hitler!*'

'*Heil Hitler*,' Delsingen responded. He did not raise his arm, and his eyes surveyed the other man neutrally.

Mindenhof strutted out, face still pale with fury.

'And you, my dear Delsingen,' the colonel said to himself as Mindenhof banged the door shut behind him, 'have just made yourself a dangerous enemy.'

But he did not feel unduly disturbed by this as he turned to look at the Führer's portrait.

'I must take that thing down one day,' he muttered.

2

Delsingen walked into the outer office with his cap on. Geissler was talking to a sergeant who was seated at a desk but who got smartly to his feet as the colonel entered.

'Hat on, Captain,' Delsingen said. 'We're going on a surprise inspection. At ease, Sergeant.'

The sergeant sat down again.

Geissler ended his conversation with the NCO and hurried to take his cap off a wall hook.

'I'll warn your driver, *Herr Oberst*,' the sergeant said, reaching for the phone on his desk.

Delsingen paused. 'No. Captain Geissler will drive. Have you the spare keys?'

'Yes, *Herr Oberst*.' The sergeant unlocked a drawer and took out the spares.

'Give them to the captain. And where is *Leutnant* Kahler?'

The sergeant cleared his throat awkwardly. 'In . . . in the toilet, *Herr Oberst*.' He was sitting to attention now.

'Again? That man spends his life in there.'

'Yes, *Herr Oberst*,' the sergeant said, then correcting himself hastily, '. . . I mean, no, *Herr Oberst*!'

'I'd give up, if I were you, Sergeant. You're digging yourself in deeper.'

'Yes, *Herr Oberst*!'

'Tell *Leutnant* Kahler where we've gone when he finally gets out of there. If anything of operational urgency occurs while we're out, he is to contact me immediately on the radio, then inform Major Mindenhof.'

'Yes, *Herr Oberst*! May I ask where the inspection is to be? So we know where . . .'

'It would not be a surprise, would it, Sergeant? And you never know, someone might warn the unit concerned.'

'No one would, *Herr Oberst*!' the sergeant protested.

'I'm sure of it,' Delsingen said mildly, knowing better as he continued on his way out. 'And stop sitting to attention.'

'Yes, *Herr Oberst*.'

Geissler grabbed the keys from the sergeant,

shrugged in reply to the NCO's raised-eyebrow query and hurried after the colonel.

Delsingen said nothing until they had left the building and were walking towards the Mercedes staff car.

'You are full of questions, Geissler?'

'The colonel will tell me when he is ready.'

'Very diplomatic.'

'I take it we're not going on an inspection.'

'Not immediately. Has Kahler always been prone to going to the toilet?'

'He was at Narvik, sir.'

'Yes, I know. I've studied his file. I was at Narvik too. I was a major then. That first German defeat was a psychological shock for many. But then the enemy was rather more ferocious than those we had previously been accustomed to. Do you think Kahler is now permanently frightened? Is that why he visits the toilet so often?'

'I would not like to say, Colonel,' Geissler offered cautiously.

'I understand.'

'Shouldn't we have a motorcycle escort, sir?' Geissler went on, wanting to keep away from the subject of Kahler's fading courage. 'For wherever it is we're going?'

The colonel did not seem to mind the change

of subject. 'We're not going far. Besides, I don't think Ålvik and his gang are close enough to shoot at us. Do you?'

Geissler looked about him. There were more soldiers about than civilians. Sandbagged gun emplacements were dotted all over the place. Some were anti-aircraft cannon.

A four-man squad of Mindenhof's newly arrived SS men, all in black uniforms, marched towards Bryggen, Bergen's old Hanseatic quarter, weapons slung. They carried brand-new MP40 sub-machine-guns, with the 'broom handle' folding stock. Hanging at each hip from the black leather belts about their waists was a leather triple-pocket ammunition pouch. Each pocket held a spare thirty-two-round magazine, to complement the one already loaded into the gun.

Because of the antipathy which existed between the Wehrmacht and the SS – the former was determined to retain military control over the latter – much of the equipment passed on to the SS tended to be of inferior quality. The SS, however, had other ideas. Already running what was virtually its own shadow industry, the organization was beginning to manufacture its own equipment. It also modified and improved upon captured enemy weaponry, which was sometimes of a better standard.

Looking at the squad's new guns, Geissler wondered where Mindenhof had 'acquired' them. He was certain they had not come through normal channels.

He glanced at Delsingen to check his superior's reaction; but the colonel appeared not to mind.

The SS men ignored every Wehrmacht uniform they passed, including junior officers. They took notice only when they saw the colonel as they stomped past. Four arms shot out.

'*Heil Hitler!*' they barked in chorus.

Delsingen raised a hand to them. They marched on.

'They still refuse to salute you properly, sir,' Geissler observed.

'Let them have their day,' the colonel said mysteriously.

He glanced to his right, at the commandeered hotel that served both as headquarters and sleeping accommodation for the SS contingent. It was festooned with swastika banners and emblems. In its immediate vicinity, a rash of posters had been put up. Some were portraits of Hitler. Others carried exhortations to greater effort for the glory of the Reich, or warnings of severe punishment for those who gave aid and comfort to the resistance movements.

One, particularly ominous, was in Norwegian, but carried the date and originating department in German. *Oslo, den 22 Juni 1941. Der Reichskommissar für die besetzten norwegischen Gebiete.* It was a brand-new poster, and was signed 'Terboven'.

Most of these warnings promised the penalty of death.

Another poster, also in Norwegian, exhorted young men to join the SS. The ghostly head and shoulders of a helmeted Norseman was flanked by the modern one of a soldier in an SS helmet, looking suitably square-jawed.

Nordmenn, it seemed to shout. *Kemf for Norge!* Norsemen. Fight for Norway!

A swelling roar made Geissler look up. A pair of Messerschmitt Me-109s hurtled past, coming from the direction of Mount Fløien, which overlooked the city, and heading out along the fiord. Soon, they had disappeared.

'Hunting for straying Tommis, no doubt,' Delsingen remarked without looking up. 'If they're mad enough to come all the way here.'

Geissler hurried on ahead as they approached the car, to open the passenger door, but Delsingen stopped him.

'Get behind the wheel,' the colonel said, then opened the passenger door himself and got in.

'How far is "not far", sir?' Geissler asked, as they shut the doors. He put the key in the ignition.

'Just follow my directions.'

Geissler started the car and they moved off.

'Here. This will do. Stop here.'

Geissler brought the car to a halt, in response to Delsingen's command.

'Let us walk,' the colonel said, and climbed out. 'Bring the radio.'

Geissler pulled the bulky handset out of its base unit beneath the instrument panel. The radio was in a camouflaged canvas pouch with a rolled sling tucked into a side pocket. He got out, unrolled the sling and slipped it over his left shoulder.

They had stopped at the end of a road that had coursed its way up Mount Fløien. Close by, was the penultimate stop of the funicular railway that began on the Øvregaten and went up to a mountain-top restaurant. The upward car, full of off-duty soldiers, had stopped. But they did not make for it.

The colonel strode off up the mountain, with

Geissler in tow. They passed gun emplacements, several of which were multi-barrelled
anti-aircraft cannon. The soldiers and junior
officers manning them snapped to attention,
clearly wondering whether the colonel had
come on a sudden inspection. He was not
their commander but, like soldiers everywhere,
they had long ago come to the conclusion that
the presence of any senior officer always meant
a disruption of their daily routine. Then they
relaxed as he went on, relieved to discover they
were not the object of his visit.

Delsingen and Geissler kept walking until
they reached the last stop. The restaurant,
looking like a miniature palace of crystal and
wood, came into view. It sat atop the mountain,
looking down on the city spread below. It was
doing good business. The uniformed diners
were all officers from the various services.
Two of the anti-aircraft weapons were sited
in the grounds.

'This mountain is bristling,' Delsingen
remarked. 'Hartmann and his boys intend
to shred any enemy aircraft that ventures
this way.'

Hartmann, also a Wehrmacht colonel, was
in command of the local area artillery.

A path which skirted the restaurant led to its

terrace. Delsingen paused there by the safety railing, and stared out over the city. They were now just over a thousand feet up. He looked down at the E-boats moored in the inner harbour, and at the other craft further out. An E-boat was going out on patrol, streaming a white, boiling wake that churned the surface of the water.

'The city among the seven hills,' he began quietly. 'Before the war, my wife and I came here for our honeymoon. Germans have been coming here for a long time. Since the early thirteenth century there have been German traders in Norway, followed a century later by the Hanseatics. And now . . .' Abruptly, he continued walking, crisply returning a salute from two passing soldiers. 'Come, Geissler.'

They continued beyond the restaurant, using an easy trail that took them further up the mountain. At last Delsingen stopped. They were well clear of the restaurant, with a spectacular view of Bergen, the surrounding mountains and the fiord and skerries. There were no soldiers or gun emplacements within 300 yards.

'We can talk,' the colonel said. He did not look at his subordinate.

Geissler took a nervous glance about him, as

if expecting to see Mindenhof suddenly materialize. He waited for the colonel to continue.

'Don't look so worried, Geissler,' the colonel said, his eyes still on the city below. 'Mindenhof's snoopers are a long way from us.' Delsingen placed his hands behind his back as he stared down at the city. 'We are going to lose this war. We began losing it the day *Adler Tag* failed. The Tommis, as you know, call it the Battle of Britain.'

Out of the corner of his eye, he observed the startled turning of the captain's head, as Geissler stared at him.

'It is true, Geissler. I know if our fanatical *Sturmbannführer* could hear me, he would choke on his oath to Hitler, denounce me, then do his best to have me shot as a defeatist traitor. That idiot truly believes in the thousand-year Reich. We have sown the wind and one day the whirlwind will be upon us. And then, Geissler, we shall pay. How we shall pay.' The colonel spoke softly as he continued to look down on the city, given a cloak of peace by the distance. 'My wife and I were truly happy here.'

Geissler said nothing.

'Mindenhof has an unsavoury past in the SS,' Delsingen continued, 'even by their own standards. I am quite aware that he is ruthlessly ambitious, and will do *anything* to advance himself.'

Uncertain of how to deal with the colonel's dangerous frankness, Geissler said uncertainly, 'Strictly speaking, *Herr Oberst*, he is your second in command.'

'And a difficult one he's proving to be.' Delsingen spoke as if to himself. 'He wants nothing less than full command of the unit. I could thwart his ambitions by giving you a field promotion to major.'

Geissler's eyes twitched beneath the peak of his cap. 'If the *Herr Oberst* would permit . . . I would very much like to be a major – but not at the expense of *Sturmbannführer* Mindenhof.'

'It would not be at his expense. You'd be of equal rank.'

'He would not see it like that.'

The colonel smiled tightly. 'You are a cautious man, Geissler. Good.'

'Was that a test, *Herr Oberst?*'

But Delsingen made no reply. Instead, he continued, 'Today, Geissler, Operation Barbarossa has begun. It is madness, of course. We are striking at the Soviets, hoping for a swift blitzkrieg victory, while still heavily engaged in the west. When the Japanese attack the Americans – as they most certainly will –

we shall have the Yankees fully in the war,
with all the weight of their industrial might
against us.

'It is what Churchill hopes for, and he will
get it. I tell you, Geissler, we shall truly pay
a terrible price for our folly, no matter how
long it takes. The thousand-year Reich will be
expensive in blood, and will not last beyond
this war. I am not the only one who has come
to that conclusion.'

Delsingen at last turned to look at the
dumbstruck captain.

'You are wondering,' the colonel said,
'whether I am mad to talk to you like this.
You are perhaps asking yourself: how do I
know I can trust you?' He paused. 'I know
more about you than you think. Mindenhof
is not the only person out here with powerful
contacts. I have a close friend in the SS. We
were at school together. He now holds general
rank – *Gruppenführer-SS*. When he heard I had
been given this command, he came to see me.
He wanted me to keep an eye on you.'

Geissler's expression had turned to one of
alarm. 'On *me*?'

'Don't worry, Geissler. You are safe with me.
You will receive no attention from the SS. But
perhaps *you* can now feel you can trust me

sufficiently, and can tell me about that young woman you walked away from.'

For several moments, Geissler said nothing. 'The *Gruppenführer* you mentioned, sir,' he was at last able to say quietly. 'He *knows*?' There was a tinge of real fear in his voice.

'You know what the SS are like. They check up on everybody. However, as a favour to me, the information he gave me is not listed in your files.'

'So Mindenhof . . .'

'Knows nothing of it.'

Geissler gave a hesitant sigh of relief. 'I do not feel proud of what I did,' he began, a sense of guilt now in his voice. 'She was so beautiful. The most beautiful . . .' He stopped, remembering. 'This is what they have done to us,' he continued bitterly. He shook his head. 'No. This is what we have done to ourselves. We allowed it. Her father was my music professor. I frequently dined at their house. That was how I met her. I could not believe anyone could be so beautiful. She was . . . ethereal . . .'

'And you stopped seeing her, because she was a Jew.'

Geissler turned to look out on the city below. There was a suspicious glisten to his eyes. 'To my eternal shame, yes, *Herr Oberst*.'

'Do you know where she is now?'

Geissler shook his head slowly.

'Perhaps you will find her again,' Delsingen suggested.

'She may already be dead.'

'Will you look for her? Is there enough of the man left in you to try? Just in case?'

Geissler was again silent for several moments. 'If I ever get the chance, I shall,' he vowed eventually. 'I might never find her again. I'm . . . I'm not sure I deserve to. But I will at least try to find out what happened. I owe that to her – and to myself.'

'Good,' the colonel said. 'Now I shall tell you what I intend to do about Ålvik. First, we will prevent Mindenhof from taking out his frustrations on the local populace.'

'He won't like that. He'll bring in more SS personnel.'

'He'll try. He does not know I have my own big gun in the SS. All his requisitions will be seen by my old classmate.'

'He won't give up.'

'I am well aware of that. However, I intend to have Ålvik neutralized, before our *Sturmbannführer* can whip up sufficient support for his requests. There will be plenty of people out for revenge on us, when this war is over. As long as I am responsible for this unit, no one under my command will be allowed to abuse the locals. I will be ruthless in hunting out Ålvik's gang, even though I fully understand his reasons for attacking us. He is fighting for his country, and it is our job to stop him; but I will not use the local civilians as hostage fodder.'

'Many of them support him, and others like him.'

'If they're caught with weapons they are no longer civilians but soldiers, and must accept the fortunes of war. Until that occurs, none of the locals will be terrorized.'

'What about the members of the Nasjonal Samlig, the Hird, and the Bergen detachment of the Germanske-SS Norge? Mindenhof calls them his "sympathetic" Norwegians.'

'He's used that same description to me.'

'These particular Norwegians, sir, are sometimes harder on their own than even Mindenhof.'

'The convert always wishes to prove himself, and is frequently more brutal. The classic lesson of occupying a country, Geissler. Caesar employed the tactic centuries ago. When he had raised his legions among the conquered, he sent them out to pacify other nations. His Teutonic legionaries did their fair share.

Nothing is new, Geissler. Only the methods, and their implementation, change.'

'*Herr Oberst* . . .' Geissler said, '. . . do you really think Barbarossa will . . .?'

'Fail?' Delsingen supplied. 'It is inevitable. The Führer and his advisers have seriously miscalculated. Oh, our blitzkrieg will certainly stun the Russians and we shall make great advances – initially. I also suspect that our troops, and their Waffen-SS comrades, will not be gentle with the populace, whom they will look upon as sub-human. More acts to be avenged by the Russians. When the enemy finally rallies, he will come at us in great hordes.

'They will get better and better, Geissler. They will be fuelled by a great hatred and anger; and to help them, they will have the force that took such severe toll of Napoleon's troops: Generals January and February. Some leaders never seem to study history closely. If they did, it might help them avoid the more glaring of their mistakes; and people like us would not have to be sacrificed to their vanity. Our forces are fighting on several fronts, against a mass of enemies who will eventually overwhelm us. The people of the countries we have occupied will have their revenge one day; perhaps sooner than our great Führer and his Mindenhofs think.

The Fatherland, inevitably, will suffer gravely for this madness. A few of our countrymen can see it; a very, very few.'

Geissler was again looking anxiously about him.

Noting this, Delsingen said, 'You are disturbed by my comments. More than ever you think I am mad to say these things, even up here on this mountain.'

'I am worried for your safety, Colonel. Ålvik's people are not the only snipers.'

'Even Mindenhof would not be so blatant as to attempt to assassinate me openly. The man is an appalling example of German manhood, but he is not stupid.'

'He would blame it on terrorists.'

Delsingen waved an arm briefly, indicating the immediate area about them. 'This mountain is crawling with Wehrmacht troops. Ålvik's people would not be so insane as to come within five kilometres. If Mindenhof has something in mind, he will be far more subtle. When I called him an idiot earlier, I meant it as a comment on his philosophy, such as it is.

'He is dangerous, but he is also sly. When he was a captain, he got rid of a rival of equal rank by sleeping with the man's wife. The enraged husband, not knowing the identity of the man

who had cuckolded him, shot the wife. He
was executed for the murder. It was his great
misfortune that the wife had also been the
daughter of the local *Gauleiter*.'

'If you know so much of Mindenhof's personal history, sir, it's all the more reason for
you to be careful. He will be constantly seeking
ways to discredit you.'

'I have been given command of a unit,'
Delsingen said calmly, 'that is distinct from the
other forces in the area. This gives me a certain
degree of autonomy. Don't worry, Geissler. I
know my enemy – both the Norwegian and
the German. And I will face both, when the
time comes.'

They set off back down the mountain.

'We had better inspect some poor unit,'
Delsingen said, 'to satisfy Mindenhof's inevitable curiosity.'

The radio remained silent.

Whitehall, London, the same day
In a small office whose shabbiness belied
its importance, two men in crumpled suits
sat facing each other, at two desks that
had been pushed together. One was staring
with open disbelief at a sheet of paper he
had picked up from a pile that a secretary

had recently brought in. He pursed his lips thoughtfully.

'Look at this,' he said to his companion, passing him the sheet.

The other man took it, read slowly, then read it again.

'Well?' demanded his colleague.

'I find that hard to believe . . .'

'My feelings precisely.'

'However, it would be prudent to keep an eye on developments. The source appears to be one of our more reliable ones.'

'He could have been compromised, and Jerry's put that out to confuse us.'

'He would have slipped in a warning with the code. If he had been unable to transmit himself, he would have left something out. That would also have warned us. And yet . . .'

'And yet?'

'One can't really hide a battleship, even when it's only just being built. According to this, the keel's barely laid. It could be a hoax. They may not intend to build it at all, assuming the keel-laying is the real thing.'

'What should we do?'

'Wait and see if anything further comes in on this.'

But the men in the shabby room would

hear nothing further of the phantom pocket battleship – the *Graf von Hiller* – for another three years. During that time, with other, vitally urgent matters constantly vying for their attention, they would forget all about it.

Until it was too late.

An envelope with a bright-red seal was waiting for Delsingen when he returned to his office after his perfunctory troop inspection. He stared at it as he placed his cap, with studied deliberation, on his desk. He picked up the square, buff envelope. Apart from his address, there were no markings except for the dried wax of the seal. He recognized the stamped insignia.

He inspected the envelope minutely, checking it for tampering, then smiled grimly. No one would be daring or suicidal enough to interfere with the *Gruppenführer's* communications.

Delsingen began to unseal the envelope. He took the single sheet of paper out of it, then went round to his chair and sat down. He began to read:

My dear Rüdi,

A request from Mindenhof has landed on my desk. He has asked for an additional two SS officers, two *Unteroffiziere*, and 20 men. Do you approve of this? It is clear he has not informed you, for the request came through SS channels. I will do nothing until I hear from you.

    Max

The colonel gave another grim smile as he finished reading. Mindenhof was already attempting to bolster his forces.

'*Geissler!*' Delsingen shouted.

The door opened almost immediately. '*Herr Oberst?*'

'Come in, Geissler. And shut the door.'

The captain obeyed and walked towards the desk.

'Read this,' Delsingen said, handing him the letter.

Geissler took it wordlessly and began to read. His eyes grew round as he took in its meaning.

'My God, sir,' he said, returning the paper. 'He must have put in that request some time ago. Everyone knows how long it takes for something like this to get through.'

'Obviously not in the SS,' Delsingen said drily. 'Not one for letting the grass grow under his feet, our *Sturmbannführer*. He is greedy, but sly. He's trying to build up his own SS forces. However, he's doing it gradually, hoping that by the time he feels he has a sufficient number it will be too late for the poor fools in the Wehrmacht to do anything.'

'Is this from the, er, person you spoke of, sir?'

'Yes.'

'What are you going to do?'

'Promote you to major. I need two deputy commanders.'

Geissler looked white around the gills. 'Is that such a good idea, Colonel?'

'Calm yourself, Major. Your record shows you're an excellent man in combat. Mindenhof is only human.'

'There are many descriptions in my mind for him,' Geissler said. 'Human isn't one of them.' He was quite serious.

'All the same, you are now a major. I'll see that the promotion goes rapidly to the High Command, for approval. With my recommendation tagged to it, consider the rank confirmed. Before this war is over, Ernst,' Delsingen went on, 'you will see many terrible things – perhaps do some yourself – and face up to terrible nightmares. If Mindenhof is one of those nightmares, so be it. Any objections, Major?'

'Er . . . no, *Herr Oberst*,' replied a stunned Geissler.

'Good. Get yourself some new insignia. Tomorrow, I shall be calling a special meeting, with certain officers from both the Luftwaffe and the Kriegsmarine in attendance. You and Mindenhof will be there. I expect to see you in major's uniform.'

'Yes, sir!'

'Thank you, Major.'

South-east England

The two Spitfires came in fast and low over the grass strip, flitting shadows in the late-afternoon sun. The wingman performed two slow rolls.

'Oh dear,' remarked a pilot, lounging on the ground with his Mae West on. 'Jo-Jo hasn't scored, while young Bede has. This will not please our Antipodean.'

'It's not that he isn't good,' another said thoughtfully, as they watched the Spitfires come in to land. 'We've all seen him in a fight. He's ferocious . . .'

'But a terrible shot,' a third put in.

'It's just bad luck,' the first pilot said. 'I once saw him glued to the tail of an Me-109. Whatever that Jerry did, he couldn't shake off old Kearns. He was a dead duck. No more *sieg heiling* for him. No more *"Jawohl, mein Führer!"* or whatever it is they say to that lunatic with the toothbrush moustache. But poor old Jo-Jo's guns just wouldn't fire. For a moment, I thought Jo-Jo was going to ram him in frustration. In the end, I had to put the Jerry sod out of his misery, when Jo-Jo called for me to administer the old *coup de grâce*. When we landed, Jo-Jo was fit to bust, as our Yank friends would say.'

'Well, it can't be his bad luck,' the second pilot joined in. 'He's never been shot down, while all of us have.'

The three of them, on standby, were sprawled close to their machines. None had yet reached his twenty-first birthday.

'Twice for me,' said the first pilot gleefully.

'I think you bale out just for the fun of it,' one of his companions said. The third pilot. 'Anyway, I think Jo-Jo's lucky. No one who flies with him is ever shot down.'

'A flying rabbit's foot,' the first pilot said.

They laughed.

'He did get one,' the second pilot recalled. 'Some weeks ago.'

'Ah yes,' confirmed the first pilot. 'I remember. A fat old sitting duck of a flying boat, off the Dutch coast somewhere. Had to share it, though, didn't he? Who was with him that day?'

'Spots Spottiswood.'

'Alas, poor Spots. Knew him well. Bought the farm, poor devil.'

Spottiswood had been nineteen and a half years old.

'He wasn't flying with Jo-Jo that day,' the third pilot said triumphantly, seeing that as confirmation of Kearns's luck. 'He would still have been alive if he had.'

'If you say so, old son,' the first pilot said.

'I do say so. Old Spots is dead, isn't he?'

'We don't always fly with Jo-Jo. We're still here.'

'But for how long?'

No one laughed.

The mark of Spitfire flown by Jo-Jo Kearns's squadron was the Vb. The V was eventually to become the most numerous Spitfire and the Vb version, powered by a 1440-horsepower Merlin 45 engine, was armed with two 20mm cannon and four .303 machine-guns. While it took its toll of the Messerschmitt Bf-109, the Focke-Wulf Fw-190 gave it a tough time indeed. The radial-engined Fw-190 was smaller, lighter, stronger, even more powerfully armed, and highly agile. At that period of the war it was ahead of its time. A Spitfire V pilot who won against it either had to be very good, be lucky enough to catch an enemy rookie, or come up against an indifferent pilot.

Kearns had previously come up against good pilots but as his colleagues knew, he was an exceptional flyer. Most importantly, he was also very good at looking after his wingmen. There was an added bonus. They tended to score when in his company and, not surprisingly, everyone wanted to fly with him.

Pilot Officer Kearns was almost too old for the rank at twenty-one, and a bit of an enigma. Unlike the other pilots in his flight, he had begun as a sergeant, then moved up a rank to flight sergeant, before receiving a commission as a pilot officer. Though there were others on the squadron a year or two older than he was, in combat terms he was among the veterans. A Queenslander, he came from a family who were uncompromising in their hostility towards his decision to travel all the way to Britain to join the Royal Air Force.

This hostility had its roots in the family history.

The ancestor whose name he bore had been transported to Australia nearly two centuries earlier, for the heinous crime of stealing a chicken to feed his starving wife and child, who had then subsequently died during his enforced exile. He had willed himself to survive the appalling harshness of the penal colony and on eventually gaining his release in that vast, unforgiving land, had started a new family to replace the one he had lost. He never again set foot on British soil.

His descendants, who were now prosperous, were never allowed to forget how they came to be in Australia. It was burned into the family psyche. So when Johnny Kearns had announced that he was going to the old country to offer his services to the Crown, it was looked upon as the worst kind of treachery. Cutting him off from the family wealth was threatened. But Kearns had had no intention of changing his mind. With a small, secretly given sum from a sympathetic grandfather, the lonely and ostracized youngster had made his way to England.

If asked, he would not have been able to properly explain why he had been so stubborn and had chosen to estrange himself from his family, except to say that he believed in what he was doing. The family, had they so wished it, would have recognized in him the strong will of the man who had been the founder of the Kearns Australian tribe. They would have seen the spirit of the man who had not been defeated by his terrible experiences. They would have recognized a certain irony that might have given them pause for thought. But, having benefited from the wealth whose creation had begun with the reluctant convict all those hard years ago, they had chosen not to do so. Cushioned in moneyed comfort, they found it easier to milk the ancestral cross they bore for all it was worth.

Needless to say, the young Kearns's distant forebear would have recognized himself in his stubborn descendant.

As he taxied towards the waiting ground crew, family problems were not on Kearns's mind. He was fuming. His guns had jammed yet again after one burst, just when he'd had the Fw-190 pilot where he'd wanted him. The enemy aircraft had spiralled away trailing smoke, but had recovered sufficiently to scuttle back to its base in France.

Kearns's wingman, Pilot Officer James Bede – whom everyone had taken to calling 'Venerable' – had scored two kills. One had been against a Ju-87 Stuka that had been damaged during an anti-shipping strike in the Channel. The other kill had been the Me-109 that had been shepherding it home.

Kearns, having set Bede on the Stuka, had gone for the 109; but the Fw-190 had made an unexpected appearance, very determined to join in the fun. Kearns had broken off his attack on the Messerschmitt, to turn to face the more dangerous enemy. Bede, having mortally wounded the Ju-87, had then engaged the 109 that Kearns had been forced to abandon. By the time Kearns had given the pilot of the Fw-190 the fright of his life, Bede had dispatched the 109.

'*Bloody guns!*'

Kearns's frustration was unmistakable in the yell that rose above the sounds of the dying engine as the aircraft came to a stop and he slid back the canopy. He got out and made his way to the ground in a fury.

'Jesus, blokes!' he went on to the curious ground crew who had gathered. 'What the bloody hell's going on with these guns? And don't blame it on gremlins. There's a Nazi that's alive and well today, when he bloody well should be dead! I had him. One fart from the guns, then *nothing.*'

Kearns looked as if he had the enemy pilot by the throat. His hands were curved into claws round an invisible neck which he shook once, to emphasize the last word.

'I'd have got more action from a dried-up wallaby's tits!' he went on, teeth bared in a humourless grin. 'Find out what the hell happened!' He began to stomp away from them, then stopped and turned round. 'Look,' he said more calmly. 'I know it's not your fault; but how would you feel if you'd had a 190 so close you could see the scared bastard's head in the cockpit looking back at you, scared enough to shit? Then your guns don't work.'

'Bloody annoyed, sir,' one of the mechanics ventured.

'*Annoyed?*'

'Bloody fucked-off, sir,' another suggested.

'That's more like it. I want these things

working next time I'm up. Give it a go, will you?'

'We will, sir. Bad luck, sir.'

Kearns slowly removed his helmet. 'Yeah,' he sighed. 'Bad luck.'

3

Bergen, Norway. 0800 the next day
Geissler, resplendent in major's uniform, knocked on Delsingen's door.

'*Hierein!*'

Geissler entered and saluted smartly.

'Ah, Geissler,' the colonel greeted him. 'So, how does it feel to be a major?' He'd been putting some papers into a thin blue folder.

'Getting used to it, *Herr Oberst.*'

'Thought you might,' Delsingen commented, the fasteners on the folder clicking sharply as he snapped it shut. 'Take off your hat. Relax. We have a little time before the others get here.'

Geissler removed his cap and tucked it beneath an arm. 'Didn't see you at breakfast, sir.'

'I had an early coffee. Terrible stuff. I hear the Norwegian resistance sometimes manages to get the real thing. Interesting, isn't it, Geissler? We have all the weaponry and the men. We're in control. But we can't get proper coffee.' Delsingen paused, as if remembering what good coffee was like.

'The restaurant on the mountain sometimes has the real stuff,' Geissler said.

'Yes,' the colonel said drily. 'And I wonder where *they* get their supplies from.'

'Nobody asks. Not even Mindenhof. We all like to taste the real thing now and then.'

'You see? He does have a human side.'

'I doubt it, sir. He'd close that place down out of spite, if it suited his purposes.'

'Speaking of which, has he seen your new rank yet?'

'No, sir. He'll know soon enough, if one of his cronies hasn't already passed on the news.'

'I've had the order posted.'

'I can see his face now.'

'Looking forward to that?'

'Not really, sir.'

Delsingen glanced at a clock on the wall. 'Time for the briefing.' He got up from behind his desk, picked up the folder and went to get his cap off its hook. 'They should all be there. Hat on, Geissler.'

The new major followed his colonel out of the room.

* * *

Two officers were waiting: a Luftwaffe lieutenant colonel and a navy lieutenant commander.
They snapped to attention when Delsingen
entered the room, and saluted in the standard
military manner.

'*Oberstleutnant* Gustav Mölner, Luftwaffe.'

'Korvettenkapitän Ulrich Fröhmann, Kriegsmarine.'

Delsingen returned their salutes. 'At ease,
gentlemen. Please sit down.'

Five chairs had been arranged at a large,
round table. Each visiting officer removed his
cap and placed it on the table before him, then
took his designated seat. Delsingen removed his
own cap, placed it on the table at his position,
put the folder down next to it, but remained
standing.

He looked at Geissler. 'It would appear that
Major Mindenhof is late. Find him, will you,
Geissler?'

Geissler's eyes gave nothing away. 'Sir,' he
acknowledged, and went out to find the SS
officer. He turned a corner into a short
corridor, and saw the gleaming black uniform
striding towards him. He stopped, waiting for
Mindenhof to draw near.

The SS major slowed his pace, then came to
a halt, his face expressionless.

'You're late,' Geissler said firmly.

The black eyes stared pointedly at Geissler's new insignia of rank.

'Don't feel too bold with those on, Geissler,' Mindenhof said coldly. 'I'm still senior to you.'

Geissler did not react to the taunt. 'The colonel's waiting. He is not pleased that you are late. The others are already there.'

Mindenhof's eyes glared beneath the peak of his spotless black cap. 'Don't push your luck, Geissler.'

He brushed past the army major, and continued on his way.

Geissler followed.

When they got to the door of the briefing room Mindenhof stood aside, expecting Geissler to knock.

Geissler watched him and did nothing.

Mindenhof's eyes hardened as he hesitated slightly. Then, seeing that Geissler had no intention of moving, he knocked sharply.

'*Hierein!*' came from within.

Mindenhof opened the door and stamped in, heels clicking sharply as he snapped to attention. His right arm shot out. '*Heil Hitler! Sturmbannführer* Mindenhof reporting as ordered, *Herr Oberst!*'

Mölner and Fröhmann began to get to their feet in response to the Hitler salute, but Delsingen indicated that they should remain seated.

The colonel stared at Mindenhof. 'You are late, Major. Please take your seat.'

Mindenhof stood uncertainly for a moment, temporarily confused by Delsingen's reaction. It was clear from his demeanour that the lack of response to his salute had not gone down well with him. He was also irritated by Geissler's sudden promotion, and annoyed by the public censure in front of the off-unit officers. However, he had expected a demand from the colonel that he explain himself for being late for the briefing. He had been deliberately late, and knew that Delsingen knew it. It was the colonel's low-key response to this that was confusing him.

Well aware of his own nature, Mindenhof expected everyone to be involved in a plot of some kind, and was convinced that Delsingen was planning something. This made him wary of things he could not foresee. He was beginning to realize that Delsingen was made of far sterner stuff than he had originally imagined. No matter. A Wehrmacht officer was no match for a dedicated member of the Waffen-SS.

'Major?' Delsingen was saying mildly.

'*Herr Oberst.*'

Mindenhof slowly removed his cap, walked to the table and carefully placed it among the others. The black cap, with its death's-head insignia and sweeping prow, was starkly different. Its presence dominated. Mölner and Fröhmann, glancing at it warily, appeared morbidly fascinated.

Even with an expressionless look on his face, Mindenhof still appeared to be smirking. He took his seat in a studied manner, fully enjoying the impact his presence had on the visiting officers.

'Lieutenant Colonel Mölner,' Delsingen began, introducing them, 'and Lieutenant Commander Fröhmann. Gentlemen, Major Mindenhof.'

Mindenhof nodded with cold detachment. The other two nodded at him, as they would at a dangerous beast they hoped would not attack them.

'Take your chair, Major,' Delsingen now said to Geissler, who had entered and was pushing the door shut. 'Then we can begin.' The colonel sat down.

'Sir,' Geissler said. He went to the last empty chair and placed his cap with the others on the table, then he too sat down.

Delsingen got straight down to business.

'I have been authorized,' he began, 'to form a unit whose specific task is to hunt out the resistance movements in the area. If this unit proves to be successful, it will form the basis for more units which will be deployed throughout the occupied countries. The unit which we're forming here will be the prototype. Success will mean more units in Norway. When these have also proved to be successful, the work on forming the others for the remaining occupied countries will then begin.' Delsingen paused to look at Mindenhof, whose face had gone pale and stiff. 'You have a comment, Major?'

'With respect, *Herr Oberst*,' Mindenhof said tightly, 'you also mean *future* occupied territories. Also, the SS is already responsible for . . .'

'Yes, yes,' Delsingen interrupted mildly. 'I know what you're going to say. Do not worry, Major. The normal SS role is not being usurped. As for future occupied territories, we shall know in the fullness of time what transpires. So, if you'll bear with me, I'll explain the specific role of the new unit. May I have your indulgence?'

Mindenhof's eyes tracked round, looking into the faces of the others at the table. They all had neutral expressions. The black eyes snapped back to the colonel.

'Please excuse the interruption, *Herr Oberst*.' It was not a climb-down.

'I have already forgotten about it.'

If anything, Delsingen's magnanimity annoyed Mindenhof even more. It had established the fact that the colonel was in such complete command that he could afford to be generous. Someone other than Mindenhof would have been grateful for not being bawled out in company; but to him, it was an even greater put-down, in front of everyone at the table. A knot of anger tightened in his stomach. It was an anger that would bide its time, determined to exact its revenge at the appropriate moment.

Delsingen gave no indication that he was aware of the SS officer's true feelings. Geissler, however, shot Mindenhof a wary glance, before returning his neutral gaze to Delsingen.

'To continue,' the colonel said evenly, 'we shall be forming a unified command for the unit, which is to be called *Sondergruppe-Norwegen* [Special Group-Norway] and will have the specific duty of hunting out resistance units like the Per Ålvik gang. It will deploy four-man hunter teams, and these will each have an officer, or senior non-commissioned officer, in command.

Each member will be a specialist of some kind: explosives expert, mountain trooper, sniper and so on. All will be expert in concealment.

'Each team must be able to operate independently of home base for long periods. Once deployed, they should expect to be in the field for as long as is required, to achieve an objective. There will be considerable danger. If discovered by members of the resistance, they should expect ferocious and implacable combat. In such circumstances, the options will be clear: a fighting withdrawal, and vacation of the area. While it will be hoped that such withdrawal can be achieved with the team remaining intact, it would be irresponsible of me not to warn you that this may not always be possible. If captured, *no* information – of any kind – must be given to the enemy. The general opinion is that our adversaries do not interrogate prisoners as . . . rigorously as we do.'

Delsingen paused, leaving the rest unspoken. But everyone knew exactly what he meant. If captured, the teams could expect far better treatment from their captors than any member of the resistance could hope to receive from the SS. All the military officers felt a private revulsion for the methods of the SS. None of them looked at Mindenhof. This was an act which, if anything, served to betray their thoughts more nakedly.

Mindenhof tightened his lips briefly, knowing exactly what the others were thinking. He studiously avoided looking at them, keeping his dark eyes firmly on the colonel.

'The teams' greatest effectiveness,' Delsingen went on, 'will be in remaining as difficult to spot as possible. Once discovered, their usefulness in that particular area will have been compromised. The psychological impact of these killer teams operating in the countryside will be immense. The resistance gangs will themselves feel threatened. They won't know where the next blow might come from. In short, we'll be doing to them what they've been doing to us.

'*No* contact must be made with the local populace at *any* time. The teams must not betray their presence, whatever area they may be operating in; but at least one member should be able to understand Norwegian, for eavesdropping purposes. The teams will not only be hunter-killers, but also intelligence gatherers. They will do this by observation and eavesdropping. Whenever they return to base, the information they have obtained will be absorbed into the general intelligence picture.

'If any member is injured and requires more

than basic medical attention, the team involved will contact base by a coded radio signal. Each team will have a casualty evacuation rendez-vous. These are the *only* conditions under which the rendezvous will be used and the radio operated for transmission. The radio is primarily for receiving and listening in on the Norwegian field frequencies. At all other times the teams will make their own way back to base, or to a prearranged pick-up point. There will be no exceptions to this rule.'

Delsingen now spoke directly to Mindenhof. 'Each team will have at least one member of the Waffen-SS. He may be the officer in command, or one of the team. Like the others, he will have an expert skill. No captures must be made and no interrogations will be undertaken in the field. As with the arrangements I have just mentioned, there will be no deviation from these orders.'

Mindenhof, at first surprised by what he saw as an olive branch from the colonel, was not at all happy about being forbidden to take prisoners and carry out interrogations.

'Then how are we to get information?' he asked.

'The teams will be operating in designated areas, basing their approach on information supplied by our intelligence network. Some of this will come from SS security operations. As you've also just heard me say, they themselves will be covert intelligence gatherers.'

'We all know that intelligence can change from day to day, hour to hour, minute to minute. The teams cannot transmit. Someone captured in the field . . .'

'Will, and can lie. A prisoner's information can also be out of date, or false.'

'There are ways . . .'

'We all know of those ways, Major,' Delsingen interrupted calmly. '*Sondergruppe-Norwegen* will be known for its ruthlessness in combat, *not* for its prowess at torture. I hope I have made this quite clear. I expect any SS personnel in the *Sondergruppe* to follow my orders. As the senior SS officer in my command, I also expect your support in this. You will instruct your fellow members of the SS accordingly.'

Mindenhof's eyes danced briefly. 'May we speak privately after we are finished here, Colonel?'

'Of course.'

Mindenhof gave a curt nod of thanks.

The others at the table continued to keep their expressions neutral.

Delsingen now opened the folder he had brought with him, and took out two sealed envelopes. He handed one each to the Luftwaffe and Kriegsmarine officers.

They opened the envelopes carefully, then read the contents.

Mölner looked up when he had finished. 'I have been ordered to place six fighters at your disposal. For the purposes outlined in here, I would prefer to have the Focke-Wulf 190. At the moment, we are using the Me-109.'

'Put in a requisition,' Delsingen told him. 'I am certain we can find six 190s, and their pilots, from somewhere.'

'If I can get those 190s, I'll find the pilots.'

'Then put in that requisition. I'll have it attended to.'

Mölner gave a tight smile. 'I'll do it as soon as we have finished.'

'Good. And you, Commander?' Delsingen went on to Fröhmann.

'I am to command a flotilla of four E-boats and, like Colonel Mölner, place them at your disposal.'

'Do you need anything special for them?'

'No, sir. They are well armed.'

'Including anti-aircraft?'

'Yes, sir. We have multi-barrelled cannon.'

'Good,' Delsingen repeated. 'I now come to other aspects of *Sondergruppe-Norwegen*. First, the air element. In addition to the six fighters, I have requested a Blohm and Voss 138, to replace the one in which my predecessor so tragically lost his life. His work for the Fatherland will not be forgotten.' Delsingen paused. 'Yes, Major?' he added to Mindenhof, who looked as if he wanted to say something.

'His work for the Führer and the Reich!' Mindenhof corrected.

Everyone at the table seemed to hold his breath, waiting for Delsingen's reply. His benevolent eyes looked squarely at the SS major. 'The Führer and the Reich *are* the Fatherland,' he said quietly, his tone clearly indicating that the other man should have been aware of that.

'That's what I meant,' Mindenhof said gruffly.

'Of course. Now where was I? Ah. Yes. The 138. This aircraft will belong to *Sondergruppe-Norwegen* and will be allocated specifically for the hunter-killer teams. It will be used to put them in place rapidly.' Delsingen looked at Fröhmann. 'A task it will share with your E-boats, Commander.'

Fröhmann nodded in acknowledgement.

'The remaining two 138s,' Delsingen went on, 'will continue with their normal duties.' His lips moved in a faint, brief smile. 'Despite the overwhelming successes of blitzkrieg operations – with the air elements working in support of the ground forces – we all know in our heart of hearts that, in a general sense, communications between the armed forces are limited. I am being polite.

'The Luftwaffe does not talk to the Kriegsmarine, the Wehrmacht does not talk to the SS and all four barely talk to each other. The point I'm making, gentlemen, is that poor communications have hampered many operations, as we all know. When the Royal Navy or the RAF attacks a ship, it takes a long time before that ship can receive air cover. I know of at least one that was sunk due to the fact that the Luftwaffe went in the wrong direction.'

He turned to Mölner. 'Please do not misunderstand me, my dear Mölner. I am not here to waste time scoring points off the Luftwaffe. The enemy, I am sure, has such problems too. However, I intend to show that close co-operation *can* yield spectacular results. I do not pretend that this will become as common a practice as I would like, throughout our forces. But I do hope we'll achieve some measure of it within our small group. Our various forces all jealously guard their independence; but remember, gentlemen, this is a war that will build to a terrible climax. We talk of blood and iron. There will be plenty of that to give us our fill. This is not the time for fighting among ourselves.'

Mölner nodded slowly. It was obvious from his expression that he was all too aware of the incident that had cost the ship.

Mindenhof looked as if he wanted to butt in, but made a great effort not to. The strain of that effort showed clearly on his face. The cold, glassy eyes seemed glued to Delsingen.

'We are all aware,' the colonel continued, 'that under normal circumstances anti-resistance and anti-partisan units do not receive the best equipment. They are not considered true front-line forces. Fortunately for us our *Sondergruppe*, as a new type of unit, will receive special attention. We *will* get the equipment we need. You, Colonel Mölner, will get your six 190s and you, Commander Fröhmann, will receive additional equipment as and when you decide you need it.'

Delsingen looked at Mindenhof. 'Major, in order to give us the right mix of personnel, I feel we may need a few more of your SS. Any ideas?'

Delsingen was aware that Geissler was staring at him with a wide-eyed expression that
telegraphed dismay.

'Well, Major?' he urged a suddenly thoughtful
Mindenhof.

'One officer of *Hauptsturmführer* rank,'
Mindenhof began, the barest touch of hesitation in his voice, 'a senior NCO, and ten
men should do it.'

'Good,' Delsingen said affably. 'You shall
have your captain, your NCO and your men.
Let me have the paperwork as soon as you can,
and I'll have it sent through quickly.'

'Very well, *Herr Oberst*.' Mindenhof looked
as if he expected a catch to be lurking in there
somewhere.

Geissler was still giving Delsingen glances
that, although covert, clearly indicated that
he was wondering if his colonel had suddenly
gone mad.

Delsingen ignored them.

'Our air cover,' he went on, 'will be for the
benefit of any Tommi aircraft that choose to pay
us a visit during operations. But we shall also use
the 190s in the bombing role, whenever we find
a resistance target. This could be a mountain
cabin, an arms dump – anything whose destruction will hurt. The E-boats, in addition to their

task of landing the teams, will also continue to hunt down commando vessels and submarines.' Delsingen paused briefly. 'The unit will go into immediate training. A programme has already been created, and within a month I expect to see the first teams go out. Our friend Ålvik has a nasty shock coming. Let us make sure he realizes that very soon.'

Delsingen paused again, then slowly looked at each man in turn.

'Finally, I am authorized to pass on to you information that very few people are aware of. It will not go beyond this room. There will be a field court martial for *anyone* who disobeys this order. The penalty will be as severe as you can already imagine. If any of you has any doubts, you may ask to be relieved of your command and your responsibilities before I continue.'

The kindly eyes had become so cold that even Mindenhof appeared to sit more upright.

No one spoke. Each man knew that even asking to be relieved of his command would have a disastrous effect on his career. The worst of postings would follow, as sure as night followed day.

Delsingen nodded and continued, 'This is what I expect of German officers. I can now tell you that a new pocket battleship is being built. She will be lighter but faster and more powerful than her sister ships already at sea. Her armament will be formidable. The enemy knows nothing of her existence. When complete, she will be coming here to Norway, to Sognefjord. Before that occurs, all the resistance groups in the area must be wiped out or neutralized. Security over her arrival and presence will be extreme. If we carry out our duty successfully, the Reich's most secret ship will remain secure and be able to strike at the enemy at will. The enemy must continue to be ignorant of her existence. She is the *Graf von Hiller*.'

'When will she arrive?' the Lieutenant Commander asked.

'I cannot tell you, because I don't know. It could be months. It could be years. Her deployment schedule is a matter for the Naval Staff, and is highly secret. Now, gentlemen. Questions?'

There were none.

Delsingen carefully put his cap on its hook and walked back to his desk. As he sat down he looked up at Mindenhof, who stood before him stiffly, legs apart, cap still on.

'All right, Major,' Delsingen began. 'I know

you've been bursting to have your say. Let's hear it.'

'There are many things that disturb me, *Herr Oberst.*'

'I've no doubt. Let's have them.'

Mindenhof seemed to pause for thought. 'At the briefing you appeared to suggest that we may not win this war.'

'I don't remember having said so.'

'You said this war would reach a terrible climax. We shall have our fill of blood and iron.'

'Yes, Major. I did say that. But I'm equally certain you did not hear me say we would lose.'

'It suggests that you expect us to fight for a long time. I do not agree. Our blitzkrieg will . . .'

'Have you ever been in combat, Major? I mean *real* combat. Not just suppressing an occupied populace, chasing a few saboteurs or manning concentration camps. I am talking about having your face in the mud while the world explodes around you. Or putting a hand out where a friend should be and touching what feels like a soft, warm and runny pie. Or seeing a helmet and turning it round to check who's lying next to you, to find a head in it but no body attached. Have you?'

Mindenhof was looking as if he was about to vomit. This, Delsingen thought, was odd for a man who had spent some time running the camps.

The SS major swallowed. 'I have not had that honour,' he said tightly. 'I have asked many times to be posted to the front; but I have been assured that my work is here.'

Delsingen made no comment. He knew that Mindenhof had no intention of going anywhere near a front if he could possibly help it.

'What other objections do you have?' the colonel asked.

'I do not believe that being soft with these people is the answer. One regiment of Waffen-SS would sweep these mountains of the likes of Ålvik and his kind. At the very least, it should not be difficult to perhaps have a unit of the *Germanske-SS Norge* deployed . . .'

'That is not an option,' Delsingen interrupted firmly. 'When dealing with people like Ålvik, try to remember this: they have lost everything that was dear to them. Their one driving force is a monumental hatred that pervades the very blood in their veins. Bludgeoning them will not make them easier to deal with. You merely fuel the hatred – and the determination.

'They will not be frightened of you and

sending in the *Germanske-SS Norge* will enrage them even further. They hate us; but they hate these particular countrymen – whom they look upon as the worst of traitors – even more. They will despise you and dedicate themselves to your destruction. You will not win that way, Major.

'The structure of the *Sondergruppe* has been approved by the General Staff. If you have objections, I would suggest you put them in writing and, I promise you, I will have them forwarded to the highest level. Who knows? Perhaps they will require your presence, in order that you may make those objections in person.'

The black eyes held a cold fury. 'May I speak frankly, Colonel?'

'You may, Major.'

'You have not won this. I know why you've shoved Geissler up a rank and made him a deputy commander. I'm not blind. I know what you're up to.'

'You misunderstand me, Major,' Delsingen said evenly. 'That can be a serious mistake. I am indulging you by allowing you to speak to me like this. As you've heard me say at the briefing, I believe that co-operation between the forces is vital to success. I believe we can show

how this can be of great benefit to our cause. As one of my deputy commanders, I expect you to show loyalty rather than try to undermine my command. I gave you a chance to get out. You chose not to. As you have chosen to stay I will demand, and expect, your full support. I do not intend to repeat this conversation with you.'

Mindenhof went through his vibrating routine. The eyes beneath the peak of his cap were malevolent; but he was trapped, and knew it.

'You will have my request for the additional men,' he said at last.

'Thank you, Major.'

Mindenhof's heels clicked sharply. The right arm shot out. *'Heil Hitler!'*

Delsingen nodded at him.

Mindenhof wheeled, and stamped out.

Delsingen gave a low sigh and shook his head slowly as the door shut behind the SS major. Within seconds there was a knock.

'In!'

Geissler entered, carrying a strip of paper.

'Ah, Geissler,' Delsingen began. 'You have a tortured expression on your face. What is it? Apprehension? Confusion?'

'Both, sir.'

'You think I've gone mad because I've given

Mindenhof a chance to bring even more of his SS into our midst?'

'I'm just puzzled,' Geissler replied diplomatically.

'Don't be. I know what I'm doing.'

'You do realize, Colonel, that Mindenhof really expects to have more SS than the requirement he'll submit to you.'

'Of course. That was why he asked for so few. He expects to have the others as well. The man's an empire builder. His own. The trick, Geissler, is to feed your enemy; but only enough to ease his hunger. Never make him strong enough to devour you.'

'So he won't be getting those he asked for through the SS High Command.' Geissler smiled. 'And, of course, he can't blame you. A flanking movement of some finesse, if I may say so, Colonel.'

'You may.'

'But you do know he won't give up. Don't you, sir?'

'I would be very surprised if he did,' Delsingen replied calmly. 'There are many ways of fighting a war, Geissler. Remember that.'

'Yes, sir.'

'Now what's that thing you're waving about like a white flag? A signal?'

Geissler handed over the piece of paper.

Delsingen read the signal, then put it down on the desk. A platoon of mountain troops had been wiped out.

He stood up, and went over to a large map of south-western Norway with its myriad fiords, islands, inlets and mountains. Various locations had been circled in red. He stared at them silently for a long time.

'He is clever, our Ålvik,' the colonel remarked softly. 'He knows we'll be noting the location of each attack. There's no logical pattern for us to follow. No way of knowing where he'll strike next. I'm certain he's got a map of his own on which he's putting his own marks. He'll be seeing the pattern we see. The trouble is, Geissler, we can only react to his moves – for the moment.

'Our teams must gather intelligence, to give us an edge. It will take some time to build a picture from which we can predict his movements with reasonable accuracy; but we shall do so. Your time is coming, Per Ålvik.'

For the briefest of moments, Geissler had the strangest feeling that Delsingen was actually in conversation with the Norwegian resistance man.

Delsingen turned to face his subordinate.

'Oh, and tell *Leutnant* Kahler he has command of one of the teams. Show him the training schedule. That should cure his visits to the toilet.'

Geissler's face broke into a slow grin. 'Or make it worse.'

'You never know, Geissler. This might be the making of him.'

The major's grin widened. 'Yes, sir.'

4

The small hut had been built into the rock-face. The narrow strip of roof that protruded from the towering wall was lushly covered with grass and moss. It was high up the mountain and, before war had come, might have been used as a refuge for mountain hikers and skiers. But this one was on no hiker's or skier's map. Access to it was via a secluded track that took a meandering and precipitous route.

The resistance movement had the comprehensive details of such refuges throughout Norway, many of which were unknown to the occupying forces.

Those suspected to have been discovered by the enemy, or whose sites had been betrayed by collaborators, were given a wide berth by members of the resistance. New huts, at secret locations, had also been constructed. The compromised refuges had sometimes been used by the invading forces. On such occasions many had been destroyed by the resistance – an inevitable consequence of the ambushes sprung on the soldiers who had foolishly taken shelter in them.

The hut that Ålvik and his small team now entered had, like many others, been presciently constructed, just before the war. One of the men, Olav Skjel, had remained outside to stand the first watch among the trees that totally concealed the refuge from view, even from someone watching through binoculars from the other side of the fiord which it overlooked. Skjel, having taken up his position, was equally well hidden.

Though basic, the hut was surprisingly comfortable and well stocked. There was plenty of room for four people to move around without crowding. Sleeping was done on the floor, on mattresses that looked like padded blankets but were also surprisingly comfortable.

There were two bench seats at a pine table big enough to accommodate six diners. There were also two low stools. The sleeping area was separated from the dining area by a partition that ended in a doorway, but there was no door. Instead, a heavy, lined curtain of plain, rough material hung from a pine rail. At the back of the hut a flush-fitting, removable panel in the pine wall led to an escape exit. There was no way of telling at first, or even second and third glances, that such a way out existed.

The rock-face behind the hut contained the entrance to a natural tunnel, created by an ancient fissure. This continued through the mountain for just over half a mile, until its exit opened out on to a steeply inclined, shrub-pocked scree that went down to a river. No roads or tracks led to that section of the river, which was heavily wooded on both sides. A powerful radio, used to communicate with Britain, was kept hidden in the tunnel.

Ålvik removed his flat cap, unslung his Sten gun and placed them both on the table. The sub-machine-gun was one of the many that had been supplied from Britain to virtually all the resistance movements within occupied Europe.

Although among captured weaponry many of his comrades prized the SS's MP40, he preferred to stick with the simple Sten. Despite some of its drawbacks, it was easy to repair in the field. He knew there were occasions when the Sten was prone to jam, usually at the very worst of moments; but it had never happened to him. He looked after the weapon scrupulously. His life depended on it.

Inge had followed him in. She carried one section of the mortar launcher in a backpack, a rifle in one hand and a pistol in a holstered belt. The 50mm launcher was little more than a tube with a base plate. She could assemble and dismantle it quickly, and was able to shift firing positions with a speed that always surprised her colleagues. She seldom required a ranging shot, rarely missing a target with the first round. Ammunition, she maintained, was precious and should not be wasted.

The remaining two men trailed in after her. one had the second section of the dismantled mortar in his backpack. In a hand-held pack, he carried the mortar rounds. Slung from his shoulder was a liberated MP40, for which he had plenty of ammunition. The last man carried a heavy machine-gun, as well as the team's field radio, which he had taken from Skjel, who normally carried it. Skjel, a fantastic shot, was also the team's sniper. He kept his superbly maintained rifle with him at all times.

They put their equipment down on the floor, then took seats at the table.

Ålvik remained standing. He unbuttoned his dark-green jacket of rough wool and pulled a map out of a concealed lining. They watched as he spread it on the table. Had Delsingen been there to see, he would have smiled grimly.

With a pencil that he took from a pouch on his left sleeve, Ålvik circled a spot on the map. It was the location where the mountain troops had been killed.

'If this map should ever fall into their hands,' he said, 'it will tell them where we've been, which is old news – not where we're going to strike next. I think we should stay here for a few days. Keep them guessing. In any case, we could do with a rest.'

The others nodded.

Throughout the area, the rest of his group would also be going to ground.

Ålvik looked at the faces of his fellow-fighters, who had also become his friends. Before the war, none of them had known each other. So far, the luck had been with them. Not one had even been injured while under his leadership. He wondered how long it would be before he suffered his first casualty. It was, he knew, only a matter of time before that happened.

He tried not to imagine who would be first. His eyes fell upon Inge, who was smiling at him.

Please don't let it be Inge, he prayed silently.

Then he felt guilty, and slightly disloyal. He would hate to lose any of them.

The man who had carried the heavy machine-gun, Morgens Morgensen, stood up and said, 'I need a cigarette.' He looked at the one with the MP40. 'Coming, Henrik?'

Henrik Arendt, who didn't smoke, first looked puzzled, then got up as he understood the other's motives.

'All right. Just to make sure you keep that smoke under control. You never know who might be watching.'

'They went out together, taking their personal weapons with them.

A charged silence fell as they left.

'You know why they did that, don't you?' Inge eventually said to Ålvik. She did not look at him.

He cleared his throat. 'I do?'

'Of course you do. They are leaving us together.'

'Inge, I . . .'

Without warning, she stood up in a rush and launched herself at him. He staggered back, nearly falling as her hands reached for his face, the palms clamping themselves against his cheeks. She drew the face close and kissed him urgently, almost devouring him. Then abruptly, she stopped and stood back, breathing hard, bosom heaving with the effort, her eyes burning with a wild intensity. A red bloom had appeared on both her own cheeks. She seemed barely under control.

Ålvik stared at her, mouth slightly open.

'A . . . a German patrol could come up this track at any time,' she began, the words tumbling over each other, 'and . . . we could be fighting for our lives. I have had my feelings for you for a long time, Per. We have been through many fights with the Germans. Once I saw a soldier take aim at you from behind a tree, and I knew if he got the chance to fire, you would be dead. All I could think of was that if you were killed, you would die without ever having made love to me. I couldn't bear to think about it. I brought up my rifle and shot him before he could pull the trigger. You didn't even know what had happened. Nobody did. Nobody else had seen that soldier.'

Her words ended suddenly, as if she had decided she'd said too much. Her eyes remained fastened on him.

Then she began to remove her clothes.

'What . . . are you doing?' he asked in a voice that had suddenly become hoarse. 'The others . . .' But his eyes followed each

94

item of clothing as she dropped it to the floor.

'Getting undressed, as you can see.'

'The others . . .' he heard himself repeat, as if taking refuge in the words.

'They will have moved far enough way from . . .'

'They planned this? You all planned this?'

She continued to undress. 'Oh, Per!' It was almost as if she had spoken to a child. 'No one planned anything. They know how you feel, even if you pretend . . .'

'How do they know how I feel? They're not me.'

With the necessarily dowdy clothes of resistance warfare now completely removed, he was at last able to see how truly magnificent a body she possessed. He watched, mesmerized, as she walked slowly up to him, the movements of the muscles in her legs and thighs sending a tingling sensation through him. She stopped, standing very close, but without touching. She didn't need to. He could feel the heat of her reaching out, caressing him.

'Now tell me you don't feel anything for me,' she said in a soft voice.

Then she reached for his mouth with her lips and kissed him gently. She drew back, eyes searching his face, before turning away to push through the rough curtain as she entered the other room.

He remained irresolutely where he was, listening as she moved around. Then the sounds of her movements stopped. After a short while, he went to the curtain and pushed it slightly aside. She was lying on one of the thin mattresses, flat on her back. Her legs were pressed tightly together, as if, having gone this far, she was now unsure of how to continue.

He entered the room and looked down at her. As his eyes roamed over her body, he felt a powerful arousal being born within him. It was the first time he had felt this way since he had lost Elle.

'You don't have to do this,' he said.

'I know you still love her,' she told him softly. 'But I don't mind.' Her eyes had begun to glisten. 'And now, I have made a fool of myself.'

'No, no,' he told her gently. He went over to her and eased himself to the floor. 'You haven't.'

A small trickle had appeared at the corner of her left eye. He wiped it away, then kissed the corner.

'What has happened to my brave mortar lady?'

NORWEGIAN FIRE

'I . . . I don't know,' she replied in a small voice.

He kissed her at the corner of her right eye, then on the forehead. He kissed the tip of her nose, then each cheek and finally her lips.

She gave a shuddering little sigh as her mouth opened in response. Her lips and tongue began working at first hesitantly, then with increasing passion. Her hands were once more holding on to his face, keeping his lips fiercely attached to hers.

Her body had begun to move.

With frantic hands, Ålvik began to remove his own clothes. It was not an easy task, as Inge would not let go. So he had to do it all while seemingly glued to her mouth. But somehow, he managed to get everything off and when at last he was able to bring his body against hers, she gave a little squeal that expressed both delight and eager anticipation.

He felt the burning heat of her as he lay himself gently on her soft body. But soon his own desires were bringing with them a very urgent need to enter her. He felt the legs he had surreptitiously admired for so long opening beneath him, in readiness for his entry.

And when he did, she gasped; and he felt resistance.

He stopped. My God, he thought, astonished. She really is!

'*No!*' she cried. 'Don't stop, Per! *Please!*'

'I don't want to hurt you.'

'You won't hurt me.' There was a touch of exasperation in her voice. She spread her thighs wider. 'Please,' she said softly. 'Come in.'

Sensing he would still hesitate, she placed both hands on his buttocks and pulled firmly. Already fully aroused, Ålvik felt himself responding and he plunged into her. Now driven by his own body's desires he found he could no longer stop, even if he'd wanted to. His need for her went beyond all other considerations.

She gave a sharp cry as he broke through. Then the cry turned into a squeal that turned into a sobbing little chuckle of pleasure that again turned into a squeal. From then on, they seemed to be frantically trying to fuse into each other's body. They rolled off the mattress and on to the floor, thrusting so hard at each other that they appeared in imminent danger of damaging themselves. They were oblivious to the world about them; to the hard floor of the hut; to the noises that were being forced out of them. Inge seemed engulfed by a series of continuing squeals, while he grunted like some primeval beast as he felt himself pounding uncontrollably into her. Their bodies became damp with the searing frenzy of their exertions.

Perhaps it was because they lived constantly with fear; or because of the things they had seen and done. Perhaps it was because of a deep longing for something other than the harsh realities of warfare. Whatever the reason, the passions that raged within sent them rolling and undulating all round the room.

At last, a great shudder seized her and she arched beneath him like a tautened bow, remaining in the tensed position for long, delicious moments. Then with a great lash of her body she hauled back, then slammed against him, stiffening and holding him fast within her. He strained at the wild, energetic body, feeling as if the very energies which gave him life were emptying into her. The breath rushed out of him in a tortured rasp that left him so completely spent, it was as if all his muscles had been turned into jelly. Then he collapsed on her in halting stages as, slowly, she too began to relax.

'You wanted me,' she said gently, a sense of wonder in her voice. She stroked his damp hair lovingly. 'You wanted me.'

'Yes,' he said. 'I did . . . and I do.'

She moved a thigh slightly beneath him.

The brief movement reminded him of the new stirrings she had generated within him when he'd first seen her lying on the mattress, waiting. He felt desire returning.

Some way down the track, but still in cover, Morgensen said to the others, 'I hope he's finally doing what he should have done ages ago.' He smoked his second cigarette, in cupped hands.

'He's still got Elle on his mind,' Skjel commented. 'And you shouldn't smoke any more. That stink will last for a while. Do you want some German mountain trooper smelling it?'

'They don't know about this place,' Morgensen retorted.

'Olav is right, Morgens,' Arendt said placatingly. 'Anyway, after what happened,' he went on swiftly before Morgensen could say anything, 'it's not surprising Per feels the way he does, is it?'

'I don't want to sound hard,' Morgensen said, ignoring the comments about his smoking, 'but he's not the only one to have lost. The living must go on, so we can make the bastards pay. If a new woman is in love with him, he should be smart enough to grab with both hands. Inge is a little younger, but under all those clothes I'll bet you she's one hell of a woman. He can't bring Elle back, no matter how much he loved her. But he can continue to make those animals pay a very high price for what they did. If Inge can prevent him from turning into a dried stick, that's good for us.'

'What are you talking about?' Arendt demanded. 'He's a good leader. Do you have complaints?'

'Of course he's a good leader,' Morgensen said defensively. 'But I've seen people go strange when something like this happens to them. They begin to take chances. They don't care if they die. The problem is, they risk other lives too.'

'Per's not like that. Not one member of our group has been killed.'

'I didn't say he's like that. But I don't believe in all that crap about war leaving no time for love. In war, time is precious. You should take everything you can get out of it. We've each got someone we care about. Per *needs* someone. It's not healthy for him to be feeding on himself like that. Not good for us, either, because one day . . .'

'I wonder how many people have been killed in this war while doing it,' Arendt said thoughtfully, deliberately veering off at a tangent.

'Plenty,' Skjel said, as if he'd been present on

each occasion. 'Maybe he thinks about that, and feels loving someone will make him vulnerable. Look what happened to his family.'

'As I have just said,' Morgensen told them, returning to his theme, 'he's not the only one to have lost people to the Germans. There is nothing wrong in being vulnerable. You know what you're fighting to protect.'

'So what do you want to do?' Skjel demanded. 'Go back up there and tell him to take Inge to bed?'

Arendt gave a chuckle. 'I'd love to hear his response to that one.'

They eventually returned to the hut, leaving Morgensen to take his turn on watch. He lit his third cigarette as he went to his position.

'Those cigarettes will kill you one day,' Arendt called softly after him.

'The war will probably do it first,' the unrepentant Morgensen countered. 'So why should I worry?'

'It's your funeral.'

'Lot's of funerals these days, but more dead bodies.'

Arendt shook his head, giving up on Morgensen and his smoking.

They entered the hut to find Ålvik and Inge

fully dressed and in the final stages of preparing a meal. There was nothing about the hut to suggest anything had happened. But though everyone took turns at preparing meals when they used the refuges, it was the first time they could remember seeing Ålvik helping Inge. They also noted there was quite a glow to her cheeks.

Arendt glanced at Skjel, who had a neutral expression on his face.

'Morgens will be pleased with what you've done,' Arendt said to Inge.

Colour rose from her neck to join the bloom on her cheeks as her head darted round to look at him. 'What?'

He pointed to the food. 'Cake. He likes cakes.'

'Oh,' she said faintly. 'I found some in the supplies.'

'Arendt again glanced at Skjel, who was looking at Ålvik.

But the leader had his eyes on Arendt. 'Not a word from you, Henrik,' he said sternly.

Arendt put a finger to his lips.

Two weeks later Geissler entered Delsingen's office.

The colonel was standing before the map,

looking at the circles he'd made. No new ones had been added.

'Still no information about attacks any-where?' the colonel asked.

'No, sir,' replied Geissler.

'Hmm,' Delsingen said.

'It's been remarkably quiet out there in the mountains,' Geissler went on, 'and it's giving me the shivers.'

'It's giving *us* time to get on with our training,' said Delsingen, still staring at the map. 'What are you up to, Per Ålvik?' he said to it. He turned to his subordinate. 'I can almost enjoy this. Our young Norwegian is a worthy adversary. The man *thinks*. I like that in an enemy.'

'Speaking of enemies, sir. Major Mindenhof is walking around with a face like thunder. It seems that his request for those extra SS men was turned down by the SS High Command.'

'War moves in mysterious ways, Geissler.'

'Yes, sir,' Geissler said, hiding a smile.

There were no attacks in the area for an entire month, and Delsingen's new teams completed their high-pressure training schedule.

Mindenhof's new SS additions had arrived

after all, but he was still fuming over SS High Command's initially negative response to his request. *Oberstleutnant* Mölner got his six Focke-Wulf 190s and Delsingen's replacement Blohm and Voss 138 had arrived.

Fröhmann's E-boats had practised fast deployments and had carried out random search-and-destroy missions in the fiords. One of those had actually borne fruit when they had surprised two agents from England, paddling to shore in a rubber boat. The operatives had clearly been brought over by submarine and had disembarked just off the mouth of one of the fiords. There had been an exchange of fire. Both agents were killed, and Fröhmann had lost one of his own crew. However, papers had been found which Delsingen thought would be useful in the fight against the resistance.

After studying them closely, he had sent the papers under secure cover to his friend in Berlin, the SS *Gruppenführer*. The major-general would know how to make the best possible use of the information.

Mindenhof had wanted to use the papers for his own purposes, insisting that as he was the SS senior officer on the spot, security matters concerning enemy agents were his responsibility.

'All right, Major,' Delsingen had said. '*You* explain to the *Gruppenführer* in Berlin why you thought it best to keep these papers to yourself.'

Mindenhof's objections had miraculously vanished, like snowflakes on a hot day. But he took being thwarted yet again with unconcealed bad grace.

'That man does not like you at all, sir,' Geissler said afterwards.

'Tell me something new, Major.'

'*Leutnant* Kahler.'

'If it's about his toilet training, I don't want to hear.'

'That's just it, sir,' Geissler said. 'Kahler has discovered new resources within himself. If I hadn't written his fitness report myself, I would scarcely have believed it. He's been transformed into a keen leader. He wants his team to be the first into operations.'

'And are you prepared to entrust him with it?'

'He'll surprise you. He certainly surprised me.'

'All right, Ernst. We'll follow your recommendation. Tell him to be ready to go within two days. He can have the honour of carrying out the *Sondergruppe*'s first mission.'

'I'll tell him.'

Delsingen smiled thinly. 'Perhaps I was right, after all. This could be the making of our toilet-happy lieutenant.'

'He doesn't go so often now.'

'You see? An improvement already.'

Within three weeks *Sondergruppe-Norwegen* had its first success, and first blood went to the team led by Kahler. They returned without prisoners, but with captured weapons as evidence of the kill. They had caught four members of the resistance. None, however, was from Ålvik's group. Even so, Delsingen held a small celebration.

Kahler's team had been in the field for most of the three weeks, patiently gathering intelligence and biding their time. The Waffen-SS sergeant attached to the team as his second in command had given no trouble and had supported him loyally. The sergeant, Heinz Eiche, was even fulsome in his praise of Kahler's behaviour in combat, when reporting to Mindenhof. This did not please the SS major, who came close to accusing Eiche of disloyalty to the SS.

But Mindenhof could not deny the fact that Delsingen's ideas appeared to have worked.

'So far,' he muttered to himself.

Barely a week later a second team, this time led by an SS captain, carried out a successful ambush. Again no prisoners were taken, as the resistance fighters never surrendered. The captain suffered one casualty: a man badly wounded. They got him back safely.

Five days later Delsingen got a summons from Berlin. He called Mindenhof to his office.

'I'm going to Berlin,' he said as soon as Mindenhof had gone through his usual routine of striding in on hard heels, clicking to attention and barking out his '*Heil Hitler*'. 'I'm leaving you in command, Major.' Delsingen fixed his subordinate with a hard stare. 'I expect you to carry out my orders without the slightest deviation. If any of the teams bring in prisoners, they are to be interrogated *without* torture. Major Geissler will be present at all interrogations to ensure that this rule is obeyed.'

'You're ordering him to spy on me, *Herr Oberst*?'

'No, Major. To ensure that our work is not jeopardized by any misguided policies. We are having success. This will continue. The way we handle our prisoners will pay dividends. Brutalizing them will not.'

'May I ask why the colonel is being summoned to Berlin?'

'You may. I have been summoned to discuss future developments of the *Sondergruppe* idea. Berlin is pleased with our initial successes. Let us not spoil the picture, eh?'

Mindenhof appeared to take a deep breath, as if biting back the words he really wanted to speak. His dark eyes were opaque.

'I wish you a safe journey, *Herr Oberst*. Watch out for those Tommi Spitfires.'

'Thank you, Major, I will. As of tomorrow, you have command until my return.'

After Mindenhof had gone, Delsingen called Geissler into the office.

'Keep an eye on him, Ernst. I don't want this to go to his head.'

'Yes, sir. What if you're away for longer than a week?'

'The same applies, no matter how long I'm away. Don't allow him to get his SS ordering the Wehrmacht around. He'll be tempted.'

'And if he tries to force the issue?'

'Restrain him.'

'Use *force*, sir?'

'One of the reasons I have not allowed him to build up the SS strength is for just such an eventuality. There's not enough of them around to give you serious trouble in a shooting match. The training we have put our men through has transformed them. Look at the change in Kahler. Our men can now give a good account of themselves against Mindenhof's SS. Besides, I believe those SS who are in the teams may not necessarily support any such moves he might try during my absence. Just keep on your toes, Geissler.'

'Yes, sir.'

'And I'll back up whatever action you may be forced to take, should the situation demand it.' Delsingen handed Geissler a sealed envelope. 'Keep this in a safe place. Your authority – which I've signed – is in there, should you need it.'

Geissler took it reverently.

'I'm counting on you, Major, to look after things until I return.'

Geissler nodded. 'I will.'

'Good.' Delsingen gave a grim chuckle. 'Mindenhof wished me a safe journey and urged me to watch out for Tommi fighters. I had the strongest feeling he was wishing I would meet them and nor survive the encounter. What do *you* think, Geissler?'

'I think you're right, sir.'

*   *   *

Delsingen's 138 made the flight to Berlin safely. On arrival, he was taken straight to the office of his friend, the *Gruppenführer*.

A tall, well-built man with fine blond hair and deep-blue eyes stood up from behind a huge ornate desk as Delsingen was ushered in. The room was big enough to make the desk look small. Quite a contrast with his own office in Bergen, Delsingen thought drily.

The SS major-general grinned in welcome. 'Rüdi!' He held out a hand as he came forward to greet Delsingen. 'Good to see you!'

They shook hands warmly.

'Good to see you too, General.'

'Call me Max, for God's sake, Rüdi.

'Max, you're looking fit.'

Max Honnenhausen shrugged. 'By the grace of the Royal Air Force, who sends a bomber or two or a high-flying reconnaissance Spitfire, I survive.'

They laughed.

'So, Rüdi. You seem to have excited some people in the High Command with your ideas.' Honnenhausen went to a drinks cabinet. 'Can I offer you something? I have a fine selection of "liberated" stuff: from France, Holland, Poland, Belgium, Denmark, Norway, even

from Spain during the days of the Condor
Legion. Plus, of course, our own good German
schnapps.'

'Quite a list of countries.'

'Yes. Isn't it? Sometimes, I wonder how we
were able to accomplish so much, so quickly.
Quite unbelievable how easy it was, and how
swiftly they all tumbled like dominoes in
a row.'

'They were asleep.'

'And we were very much awake!'

They laughed again, loudly.

'Now come on, Rüdi,' Honnenhausen urged.
'Make your choice. What is it to be.'

'I seem to remember, Max, you used to like
something you called nectar from Kentucky
– whiskey with an 'e' for excellent, to quote
you. You wouldn't still be jealously guarding
an ancient bottle of the stuff, would you?'

Honnenhausen feigned a pained look. 'My
secret!' Then he gave another laugh. 'Same
old Rüdi.'

'And the same old Max.'

The SS general reached into the back of
the cabinet to take out a full bottle of
the Kentucky nectar. 'A present from an
American newspaperman, in 1937. How the
world has moved since then. Yes. Today is

a good day to open it. We'll toast your
Sondergruppe for its successes, and for many
more to come.'

Honnenhausen opened the bottle with a
flourish and poured two generous helpings
into crystal tumblers, then went back to
the desk, leaving the bottle on top of the
cabinet.

He put the glasses down and pointed to a
comfortable leather armchair. 'Pull that up to
the desk. You can put your hat there.' He
tapped a corner of the desk.

When Delsingen had complied, Honnenhausen
raised his glass. Delsingen did the same.

'To friendship,' the SS general began, 'and
to the confusion of our enemies.'

'Friendship, and the confusion of our
enemies.'

They drank.

'Aaahh!' Honnenhausen said appreciatively.
'Let us hope the Amis don't make war as well
as they make this.'

'You believe they'll come in? Officially?'

'Don't you?'

Delsingen nodded. 'I do.'

The deep-blue eyes looked squarely at the
Wehrmacht colonel. 'I would say this to no
one but you. I believe it is inevitable, no

matter how hard we may try to avoid it.
But . . .'

There was a knock on the big double
doors.

'Come in!'

Both doors opened and a very beautiful young
woman entered. She wore an SS uniform, but
no badges of rank.

'Oh! I'm sorry, sir. I didn't realize . . .'

'Come in, my dear,' Honnenhausen said
expansively. 'May I present Colonel Delsingen.
Colonel Delsingen, Fräulein Trudi Deger. She
is in the documentation section, with direct
access to me. I would be lost without her
superb work.'

Trudi Deger showed a fetching pair of
dimples in her cheeks as she smiled at the
compliment.

She held out a hand, which Delsingen shook.
'Colonel.'

'Fräulein Deger, a pleasure.'

'The *Gruppenführer* is, of course, being
very kind.'

'Nonsense, my dear,' Honnenhausen said
warmly. 'Your work is quite exceptional. Now,
what can I do for you?'

She passed him the thin buff file she had
brought with her. 'A family of Jews, sir.

They were hiding in a disused farmhouse near Stolpe.'

Honnenhausen studied the file. 'Remarkable. Stolpe,' he went on to Delsingen, 'is just north-west of the city. You wouldn't think there'd be any Jews left hiding so close to Berlin.' He put down the file. 'All right, Trudi. I'll attend to it. Thank you for bringing this in.'

She smiled at him, pleased that he was pleased. 'Thank you, sir. I am happy to be of service to the Reich.'

She went out, beaming.

'I call her my *kleine Hilferin*,' Honnenhausen said when she had gone.

'You do realize, Max,' Delsingen began, 'that your little helper is absolutely crazy about you? Did you see the look in her eyes? If that wasn't adoration, I don't know what is.'

'Oh rubbish,' Honnenhausen said gruffly. 'I'm old enough to be her father.'

'If you say so. But the way she brought you that file was almost like a child bringing teacher an apple, or a kitten bringing in a mouse to lay at your feet.'

'Don't let that pretty face fool you. She's a zealous worker.'

'I don't doubt it.'

Honnenhausen took his place behind his desk and indicated that Delsingen should also sit down.

'But you didn't bring me all the way out here,' Delsingen continued, 'so we could talk about your female staff.'

'Indeed not. As I've said, your *Sondergruppe* is beginning to impress many people. Its importance to operations in Norway will increase during the coming months and possibly years. We have many secret projects that our enemies know absolutely nothing about. Naturally, we expect them to employ every effort in their attempts to discover these secrets. They will also try to destroy those that become operational, or attempt to prevent their deployment. But we will astonish them when we put some of these weapons into action. The *Graf von Hiller* is one.

'It is most definitely being built, but will not be put into service immediately and is being held in reserve, to strike at the Allies when they least expect it. It will be a formidable ship, Rüdi. It will also be a precious ship. And yours will be the task of ensuring it remains secure when it eventually moves to Norway.

From a security point of view, I have the authority to give you its projected deployment schedule. You are to plan your operations accordingly. However, you cannot discuss it with anyone, including your most trusted officers. They must carry out your orders on the understanding that you are working to a specific purpose, about which they have no further need to know. It is sufficient that your senior officers already know that the *Graf von Hiller* will be deployed to Norway. That is as far as their knowledge of this will extend, for the time being. The work of your *Sondergruppe* is therefore most important. Sabotage teams must *never* get near that ship.'

'I understand.'

'I repeat, your ideas are pleasing many people on the General Staff.' Honnenhausen's lips twitched in what could have been a smile. 'It also helps, of course, that you've got a friend high in the SS. Do this well, and you'll be a general before long.'

'General Delsingen sounds very good to my ears,' the colonel admitted, 'but at present I'm more interested in getting the job done – and doing it properly.'

'You must not fail, Rüdi,' Honnenhausen

told him gravely. 'High rank or not, I may not be able to do much to help you, if such a thing were to happen.'

'I understand that too.'

The blue eyes studied Delsingen. 'I'm handing you what the English would call a very hot potato.'

'My hands can take the heat.'

'I hope so, Rüdi. Now tell me: are you still having trouble with Mindenhof?'

'I'll always have trouble with him. Here's one person who would dearly love to see me fail. But for the moment he's containable. I've left him in command.'

'You've *what*?'

'If he makes a mess of things in my absence, it's his head.'

Honnenhausen gave a smile that developed slowly. 'You're sure you wouldn't like a transfer to the SS? You've got the kind of mind we like. People like Mindenhof are blunt-edged instruments, but you . . .'

'Oh no you don't. I'm a Wehrmacht man.'

'By that criterion, we shouldn't really be friends at all.'

'Yes. Crazy, isn't it?'

Honnenhausen raised his glass once more. 'To friendship.'

Delsingen raised his. 'May it last a long time.'

The precious American liquor slipped smoothly down their throats.

5

September 1941

The two Spitfire Vbs flew low across the Channel. Jo-Jo Kearns, newly promoted to Flying Officer, was leading. He was still lucky and Bede, also a Flying Officer, was still his wingman. One of the three pilots who had watched them return to the airfield that afternoon months before was no longer with the squadron. Two Messerschmitts had caught him, and though he'd shot down one, he had not made it back.

Kearns was still not getting as many kills as he would have liked, but at least no one had as yet shot him down. Bede's score, on the other hand, was mounting inexorably. He'd reached six, while Kearns had been forced to work hard for his three.

Bede had been offered the chance to lead his own pair, but turned it down. Kearns's luck, he reasoned, was rubbing off on him. As long as he continued to fly on the Australian's wing, he'd continue to return from missions.

Kearns was still cursed by the periodic jamming of his guns, but he had refused to change his aircraft. Despite the recurrent problem, he considered himself lucky with that particular aeroplane. It had never been hit in all the time he'd been flying it.

'She's looking after me,' he'd said when turning down the chance to fly a different Spitfire. 'I never change a good thing.'

Kearns now tracked his head upwards, checking that no enemy fighters were high up and planning to bounce them.

They were on convoy patrol, but with a flexible mission brief. Instead of having to fly a constant pattern over what looked like a traffic jam of ships, they had been given a freer hand than was customary. In reality it was a sort of loose search-and-destroy mission. They were hoping to catch a bomber or two on anti-shipping strikes. Keeping a tidy distance from the continental coast in order to avoid tangling with an entire squadron of 109s or 190s that might be sent to see what they were about, they prowled northwards. In addition to the fighters, there were also the fierce coastal flak batteries to consider.

Kearns preferred such mission autonomy. Beating a fixed pattern over the convoys was not without its own hazards. Trigger-happy naval gunners – either with poor eyesight, shattered nerves or weak recognition skills – were known to punch holes into the very aircraft that had been sent to protect them, despite having given the recognition code of the day to the ship controlling the convoy. Many a surprised pilot had landed with pieces missing from his aeroplane, even when he'd never tangled with the enemy.

Another hazard was sleep. The combination of flying the fixed pattern, the drone of the engine and the warmth of the cockpit sometimes conspired to induce drowsiness. People had been known to fly towards their death in a gentle descent into the water, before waking up in time to spot the approaching danger.

Kearns glanced over his right shoulder, to see Bede holding perfect station. They were keeping radio silence.

Bede, he thought, was a born natural; a natural pilot and a natural shooter. Give him real wings and he'd be a hawk.

Bede gave him a thumbs up.

He could imagine the younger pilot grinning in his mask. Then Bede was vigorously waggling his wings and jabbing a hand that pointed forwards and downwards.

Kearns looked to his one o'clock position. Two fleeting shapes, even lower down, virtually skimming the waves. Focke-Wulf 190s, heading up the Channel. But why so low?

There were three possibilities. They were keeping low to avoid radar and were on their own marauding mission; they were on a reconnaissance probe and staying low until it was time to climb to mission altitude; or they were ship hunting.

Kearns decided on the third possibility. This would mean they were carrying bombs – which meant they'd be temporarily slower and less manoeuvrable. Sitting ducks.

He realized that the 190 pilots had probably not seen the Spitfires, because the pursuing aircraft were themselves already so low. At that altitude there was a general greyness that served to hide the two RAF aircraft, hopefully until it was too late to be of any help to the Focke-Wulf pilots.

Still keeping off the radio, Kearns signalled the attack to Bede. Like a well-oiled machine, Bede extended station behind his leader as the

Spitfires increased speed to pursue. They were so low down that they were not getting the best out of their engines. Nevertheless, they were definitely creeping up on the enemy aircraft. At times the 190s seemed to disappear into the greyness of the water. Kearns found he had to force himself to maintain vigilance in the same direction until the indistinct shapes solidified once more.

He knew if he shifted his attention, it might take him too long to reacquire them, and that could prove fatal. If, in the interim, the 190 pilots became aware of their danger and dumped the 1000lb bombs they were carrying on ventral racks, it could turn very ugly indeed. Thus lightened and therefore regaining their agility, the 190s would climb for height while splitting right and left, to curve screaming round into a six o'clock attack from above. Definitely very bad news.

'But not today,' Kearns grunted.

He forced himself to get in very close until he could clearly see the bombs beneath the bellies of the German fighters.

He opened fire.

The guns didn't jam. The combined onslaught of cannon and machine-gun fire ripped into one of the 190s and almost immediately it began to pour smoke and pieces flew off it. It dropped sickeningly a few feet, and tipped on to a wing which drove into the water. The sudden jerk pivoted it about the wingtip, slamming the aircraft into the sea. It exploded on impact, but almost in the same instant the incipient flames were doused by a huge geyser of foaming water that rose into the air to fall back, a great white drooping curtain that collapsed suddenly about itself.

The second 190 pilot was very quick. He dumped his bomb and hauled for altitude for all he was worth. Bede shot off after him.

Curving round, Kearns went after his wingman to give him cover. Already both the Spitfire and the Focke-Wulf were rocketing to altitude.

Kearns followed, making sure he kept sight of the other two. He hoped the 190 pilot was not, even now, calling for reinforcements.

But Bede was not wasting time. He was all over the 190. Soon a plume of darkening flame was telling the story as it plunged seawards. By reacting instantly to the 190's escape manoeuvre, Bede had robbed the German pilot of the chance to settle down into the new situation. He had retained the psychological advantage rather than let it go to his adversary.

Kearns was impressed by Bede's consummate artistry as he watched the Spitfire heading back towards him. Bede approached with a flourish, doing a complete roll before once again closing up nearly on his wing. Again, Bede gave a thumbs up.

Kearns responded, and they continued their roving.

The two Fw-190s had failed to carry out their mission and would not be returning to base.

It was not a bad start to the patrol.

They came to land an hour and a half later, having found just one more target: a Ju-88. The twin-engined ship killer had been sneaking up on the convoy when Kearns and Bede had pounced.

Kearns went in first, his opening burst raking the rear fuselage and killing the radio operator-gunner in the back of the glasshouse cockpit. Then his guns had jammed.

In his frustration he'd called on Bede to finish off the bomber. Bede made two, devastating diagonal attacks which sent the enemy air-craft seawards in an expanding fireball. No one had got out. They chalked it up as a shared kill.

Kearns walked away from his aircraft, fuming

as he always did whenever he'd suffered a gun jam.

A sympathetic ground-crew corporal ran up to him. 'Look, sir. We've got some nice new Spits in. Perfect guns. Why don't you take one?'

'No!' Kearns growled. 'I'm not leaving her!'

'Yes, sir,' the corporal said, and went back to his mechanics.

'Well, Corp?' one of the mechanics began. 'What'd he say?'

'Same as usual. He's keeping his old kite.'

The mechanic shook his head in resignation. 'Crazy digger, if you ask me.'

'No one's asking you.'

'Steady on, Corp! Didn't mean anything by that. But we've taken those guns of his to pieces and put them back together again so many times, they must be the best-serviced guns in the whole RAF.'

'Yeah, I know,' the corporal agreed thoughtfully, watching as Bede caught up with Kearns and they walked on together. 'If it wasn't for the fact that everyone who's seen him in a fight says he's always in the thick of it, I'd say he had "bad finger" trouble. He even tried to ram a Jerry, once.'

'He's no coward, that's a fact.'

'So what do we do, Corp?' another asked. 'Check the guns again?'

'Check them again,' the corporal said wearily. 'Let's see what we find this time.'

They did a thorough check, and found nothing wrong.

'This bloody kite has a mind of its own,' the mechanic, smeared with oil and grease from his diagnostic probings, said with bemused frustration.

'It knows how to look after itself too,' the corporal said quietly. 'It's never been hit.'

'No wonder he doesn't want to change it. I wouldn't, in his place. Jammed guns or no jammed guns.'

'It's a funny thing, though,' the corporal said, staring at the aircraft.

'You still wouldn't get me up in one of these crates,' the mechanic said. 'Mad, all of them.'

'And how would you make Jerry pay for what he's doing?'

'That lot are *all* mad over there,' the mechanic said dismissively. 'Got to be, to follow someone like old Stickelgruber.'

'It's Schickelgruber,' the corporal corrected.

'Who cares,' the mechanic said. He stroked the aircraft as he would a household pet. 'Now be good to that nice Mr Kearns next time you go up. *Fire* those bloody guns!'

'Now who's crazy?' the corporal sniffed.

'We all are, what with this bloody war.'

'Mind what you say,' the corporal admonished sternly.

'Yes, Corp.'

The corporal fixed the mechanic with a hard gaze. 'Not some sort of Bolshie, are you?'

'Just a mechanic, Corp. Just a mechanic.'

Bergen, Norway. The same day

Delsingen was in his office, studying reports of more successes by his *Sondergruppe* teams. Since his trip to Berlin close on two dozen members of the resistance had been killed and valuable pieces of intelligence gathered. This information was being fed into the wider intelligence network, to see what patterns were beginning to emerge.

Many teams were now deployed in the field and, like a spreading infestation, were being dotted throughout the area. They were giving the resistance groups a hard time, but so far there was still no evidence that they had managed to catch any of Ålvik's people.

However, the resistance group had scored some notable successes, despite the virtual twenty-four-hour daylight of the summer, when spotting them should have been easier. With the days beginning to cool and shorten, and the first chill breezes of the winter to come making their presence felt, hunting them down would be that much harder.

The onset of winter would not hamper E-boat operations in the fiords. The natural heat field of the Gulf Stream ensured that they were kept ice-free throughout the year. This, Delsingen considered, was a valuable asset that would be of vital importance when the *Graf von Hiller* finally made it to the Sognefjord.

The one good thing, as far as he was concerned, was that Ålvik had not yet struck at any of the *Sondergruppe* teams. It was still a kind of stalemate. But the time would come. There was an inexorable momentum that made this inevitable.

Delsingen wondered – not for the first time – whether Ålvik was deliberately avoiding contact with the teams, until he was quite ready.

'It's what *I* would do,' he said to himself.

He was certain the Norwegian would by now be well aware that anti-resistance operations had become sharper.

Geissler knocked on the door and entered

carrying some papers. There was a smile on his face.

Delsingen looked up. 'More good news?'

'There's some good news, sir. But that's not what I'm smiling about.'

'Oh?'

'From time to time, I still remember the expression on Major Mindenhof's face when I told him you'd returned in one piece. He was just beginning to enjoy the taste of command.'

'But not long enough for him to do any damage,' Delsingen put in drily.

'I have to admit, Colonel, when I feel down, just remembering his face that day cheers me up again.'

'Whatever you do, don't bait him. He'll always find a way to pay you back. Now, give me the good news.'

Geissler placed the papers neatly before Delsingen. 'More successful contacts with the resistance. Four killed – theirs. Two wounded – ours. The team responsible is led by *Leutnant* Hartnitz, Waffen-SS.'

'Are they back?'

'No, sir. They made contact with Sergeant Stahlberg's team at a rendezvous, and passed on the information. The men are only lightly wounded, so they decided to remain for the full period of their mission time.'

'So Stahlberg's back.'

'Yes, sir. He has some intelligence I think you'll find interesting. It's with the other reports I've just brought in. They also captured some interesting weapons: a British Sten, a Luger pistol – most likely taken off a German officer's body – and another pistol which is of the type issued to officers of the former Norwegian Army. None of the dead carried identification.'

'That's to be expected. It's no surprise that many of their military men are resistance fighters. Such people would have no stomach for Quisling. This is the Hartnitz team's second successful intercept, isn't it?'

'Yes, Colonel.'

'That ought to please Mindenhof.'

'I'm not so sure.'

'What do you mean?'

'As one of our newer arrivals, Hartnitz doesn't seem too impressed with Mindenhof. He was already a combat veteran before he came here. Wounded in battle. He was also a sergeant before he received his commission.'

'Of course. I remember seeing that in his file. Officers do not generally impress him.'

'At least, not those like Mindenhof,' Geissler suggested. 'Do you think, sir,' he went on, 'that perhaps someone had a hand in the selection?'

Delsingen looked coolly at the major. 'What are you getting at, Geissler? Are you suggesting his posting was deliberate?'

'Well, Colonel . . . I just wondered whether someone, somewhere, might have decided to send us less fanatical members of the SS when Major Mindenhof made his request.'

'Are there such animals?'

'Who knows, sir.'

'Who indeed, Major. Hartnitz has an excellent combat record. The SS may well hate each other individually; but they hate everybody else much more. Remember that.'

'But what about your . . . friend, sir?'

'To everything in life, Geissler, there are exceptions. Remember that, too.'

'Yes, sir.'

The position had been well chosen. The lake on the northern edge of southern Norway's great high plateau, the Hardangervidda, was seventy-five miles east of Bergen. The lake itself was about three miles across at its greatest extent: small by Norwegian standards. On its western shore great towers of basalt provided perfect cover for the waiting ambushers.

They had been in place for some time, watching as the dots in the distance had grown into four perceptible shapes. The shapes were now close enough to be identified as four German soldiers.

Ever since news had come that the specially trained hunter-killer teams were operating in the area, Ålvik had responded by splitting his own group of thirty into six five-man units, widely dispersed, to hunt out the hunters. He had deliberately waited before committing them. This was the first such ambush, and it had been laid after days of shadowing the four men who now approached the water's edge.

From his position, Ålvik could not see the other members of his team. Skjel, the sniper, would give the signal with his first shot. The whole thing would have to be very quick. Skjel's job was to take out the leader with that first round. This would be followed by Inge's mortars, and they in turn would be immediately joined by combined sub-machine-gun fire, to complete the job.

As he watched, Ålvik could see that, though the soldiers moved alertly, it was clear they were not expecting an ambush at this point.

But they were not taking any chances. They walked well spread out, their guns ready for instant use. Every so often one of their number would do a scan, turning completely round as he walked, to check every quarter.

These were no amateurs.

He brought up his binoculars, making sure there would be no flash of sunlight on the lenses to give his position away. He focused on the leader, an SS officer. This was to be Skjel's target.

Ålvik watched as the officer stopped abruptly and raised a hand to chest height to halt the others. The SS man stood perfectly still, as if listening for something.

As he continued to watch, Ålvik saw the man's mouth move as he snapped out an order. Still too far away to be heard, the silent mouthings had an electrifying effect on the other soldiers. They darted in different directions and dropped flat to the ground.

What had the SS officer seen? Ålvik wondered. He was certain none of his own team had betrayed their position. Perhaps it was simply a soldier's instinct, warning the German that something was wrong.

Ålvik hoped Skjel would be patient and not give the game away by firing too soon.

Tense minutes passed. The very air seemed to be holding its breath.

The Hardangervidda was full of wildlife, from the lemmings to the owls that fed on them, to reindeer. But Ålvik had chosen a location where there were no deer, whose skittishness could have warned the soldiers that there were other presences in the vicinity. There were no lemmings, or owls either. So what had spooked the soldiers?

The wait continued.

A good half-hour passed before the soldiers cautiously got to their feet. They came on, but this time they ran at the crouch, darting for cover one at a time, making it difficult for Ålvik's group to catch all four exposed.

The SS officer was not sure there was anything amiss, Ålvik decided; but the man, a lieutenant and clearly a veteran, was taking no chances.

Ålvik was relieved that Skjel was being patient. The ambush site had been chosen with several options in mind. The tactics now being employed by the soldiers had been envisaged. It would merely mean that the attack, when launched, would have to be overwhelming in its surprise and devastation. The men out there would be exceedingly dangerous close in, and if one escaped being hit he would be close enough to inflict some damage.

There was a point of no return when they would have to cross open ground, and at that time it would be equally dangerous for them to retreat. That was the moment that Ålvik expected Skjel to open fire.

The soldiers continued to dart forward, never running in one direction for more than a second.

Still no firing came to crack across the stillness of the Hardangervidda.

Then the SS officer began his dash across the short stretch of open ground that skirted the edge of the lake, from where he'd begun his run.

The sharp bark of Skjel's rifle coincided with the officer's sudden jerk into an upright position. The man's arms flew outwards, his MP40 flying out of his hands and high above his head. His helmet sailed after the gun, while his legs continued to propel him forward until they suddenly lost motive power. He pitched forward brokenly, folding as he did so, and tumbled to the ground. He did not move again.

Even before the SS man had begun to crumple, Inge's mortars straddled a low rock behind which another soldier had taken cover and was in the act of rising to his feet. He disappeared in a starburst of flame and pieces of shattered stone.

Ålvik, having already picked his own target, raked the position of the third soldier. But the man had moved and was in the act of darting for new cover.

Skjel's rifle barked again, across the roar of a second mortar barrage. The soldier kept running and Ålvik thought Skjel had somehow missed.

Then the soldier stopped, stood for a moment and finally toppled.

Ålvik swung his gun to where he knew the last soldier was hiding. He was joined by Morgensen and Arendt. In the midst of all that confusion, the last man suddenly stood up and began firing back at them.

However, this astonishing display of bravery ended very suddenly as he became the focal point of the fire from the three sub-machine-guns. He was thrown rearwards, back-pedalling as he went, until he was stopped abruptly as he slammed into a large boulder. His body slid tiredly down to a sitting position, and remained where it had fallen.

The sounds of firing died in a perfect cut-off, as if a conductor had waved a baton. No one moved. Moments passed as from their positions they all stared at the bodies, waiting to see if there would be any surreptitious movement.

But there was none.

Whitehall, London

At the very moment that Ålvik's people were wiping out SS Lieutenant Hartnitz's team, the two men in shabby suits were studying a signal that had come to them via agents in France. The signal informed them that news had come from Germany of a highly secret ship that was being built.

'Do you think Jerry's having us on?' one said. 'This is the second mention of this so-called ship.'

'We feed him duff gen. His intelligence boys do the same to us. The trick is knowing when it's duff.'

'That's why we get these things. Our job is to spot the duff ones.'

'I say we file it until we get some more. There's no location mentioned. Which shipyard, for example? We can't ask for a PR Spit to wander across the Fatherland and get some poor chap shot down for nothing. PR Spits are worth their weight in gold. Can't waste them, old boy. Can't waste pilots, either. We need more specifics. Where is it being built? What class?

How far advanced is its construction? Where will it be deployed? And so forth.'

'Perhaps we'll hear from our man again.'

'If he's still alive.'

Bergen, Norway

Five days later Geissler entered Delsingen's office. He looked sombre.

'Hartnitz's team did not make the rendezvous, Colonel. Of course, they could be making their own way back independently.'

Delsingen rose slowly from behind his desk and went over to the map. Blue circles had joined the red ones, marking the locations where the *Sondergruppe* had scored kills. There were several, and they were rapidly encroaching on the red ones of the resistance strikes.

Delsingen drew a large circle with a forefinger. 'They were operating in this area. They met up with Sergeant Stahlberg's team here . . .' He paused. 'I wonder.'

'Wonder what, sir?'

'Whether they ran into Ålvik.'

'The last we heard of Ålvik,' Geissler said, 'he was nowhere near that area.'

'That was some time ago,' Delsingen said, continuing to study the map. 'He's been biding his time, as we know. In his place, I would strike where least expected.' He turned to face Geissler. 'We expect to take casualties. But I'd like to think this has not happened to Hartnitz. Keep me informed.'

'Yes, sir.'

Kiel, Germany

A senior officer in the Intelligence branch of the Kriegsmarine was in a small, dimly lit office, studying the projected plans of the formidable new pocket battleship, the *Graf von Hiller*. It was, he decided, even more powerful than the massive *Tirpitz*, which was much bigger and a ship of the full battleship class.

Though the vessel was heavily armoured, the *von Hiller*'s sleek design and potent new engines could, according to the plans, propel it through the water at thirty-eight knots. This was faster than the *Tirpitz* and almost matched the speeds of the best of the Allied destroyers, the only ships which would be able to chase her.

This would hardly do them any good, as she would be able to blast them out of the water before they could come within the range of their own puny guns. Torpedoes wouldn't be of much use, either, for in a straight dash at high speed she would outrun anything they currently had in their stocks. Hunting her down would thus be a hopeless task for either torpedo-launching surface ships or submarines. She would first have to be ambushed; but even here, the Allied forces would face supreme difficulty. The *Graf von Hiller* would have the most advanced submarine-detection equipment ever seen.

That left aerial attack.

The naval officer smiled grimly. Again, the Allies would be in trouble. The *von Hiller*'s armament was awesome. To handle surface vessels, shore targets and aircraft, she had six fifteen-inch and fourteen 5.9-inch guns; sixteen 105mm cannon; sixteen 37mm cannon; twelve Oerlikon cannon; and to round it all off, a further thirty-six 20mm cannon. Any aircraft foolish enough to come within range of the barrage that she could put up would be vaporized in the hell it would be flying into. Submarines would be no better off, for the *von Hiller* would also carry a huge supply of depth charges more powerful than anything currently available to either side.

Deployment plans were for the ship to use the Sognefjord in Norway as its base, from where it would emerge, a fast predator of the seas, to wreak havoc upon Allied shipping before returning to its lair to restock and start all over again.

The naval officer felt pleased with himself. Much of the ship's armament fit had been the result of his own proposals.

'God help you, Tommi,' he said quietly, 'if you try to destroy this ship.'

He could almost feel sorry for them.

6

Jo-Jo Kearns was lounging in the September sun, outside the squadron hut. An unfamiliar sound made him look up alertly. Was this an attack? He was not due to fly and did not have his Mae West to hand. Even so, he instinctively glanced towards his aircraft, wondering how long it would take him to sprint for it.

But the sirens weren't going, and no one was yelling 'Scramble'.

Then a sleek, twin-engined shape banked steeply as it went into a fighter break, displaying its RAF roundels, its Merlins roaring exhilaratingly.

'What the hell's that?' Kearns yelled to no one in particular.

'A Mosquito, you ignorant colonial,' someone replied cheerfully from within the hut. 'I'd love one of those.'

'Good luck to you,' Kearns retorted. 'Give

me my Spit any day. Anyway, what's this . . .
Mosquito doing here?'

'Hang on. I'll just ask my friend the Air
Marshal at the Air Ministry. He always tells
me what the brass are planning.'

'Funny man.'

'You did ask.'

'I'm regretting it already.'

Laughter came back at him.

The Mosquito didn't land. It did a few circuits,
then went on its way. Later Kearns was told that
it had been on a training flight. Despite himself,
he found his mind lingering on the elegance of
that shape and the sound of its engines.

Within a day he'd forgotten about it, never
imagining that just under three years later he
would find himself flying one, on one of the
most terrifying missions of his life.

Bergen, Norway. Two days later, 0900 hours
Delsingen strode into his office wearing a
camouflaged combat smock over his tunic.
In one hand he carried his steel helmet; the
other held an MP40 sub-machine-gun. His
pistol was belted over the smock. A pair of
binoculars hung by its strap from his neck.
He went across to his desk and put down
the helmet and the gun. He then removed

his cap and hung it up, before walking over
to the map.

Geissler, in standard uniform, came in soon
after.

Delsingen tapped at the small lake where
Hartnitz's team had been ambushed.

'This is the nearest body of water big enough,'
he said, as Geissler approached. 'It's also within
the area that Sergeant Stahlberg's team made
final contact with Hartnitz. The 138 can
land there.'

'I still think you shouldn't be going, sir,'
Geissler advised. 'The place could be crawling with resistance fighters. You don't need
the risk.'

Delsingen turned. 'I've got to go, Ernst. It's
been a week. I'm certain this one's Ålvik's.'

'But sir, you can't go into the field every time
we lose a team . . .'

'That's not my purpose. I want to see where
Hartnitz was ambushed. I want to see if my
theory is correct. I believe I understand how
this Norwegian's mind works. This is a man
who is not only very daring, but also extremely
professional in the tactics he employs. Whatever
his pursuits before the war, he has learned very
quickly how to apply his mind to the current
situation. A man who can enter the very heart of

enemy territory to exact his revenge on the man
who betrayed his family, and get out again, is no
ordinary fighter. Once I have seen the site of the
battle, I'll know whether it was Ålvik or not.'

Geissler decided he was never going to change
Delsingen's mind.

'I don't expect this to take very long,'
Delsingen continued into Geissler's silence.
'We should be back by 1500 hours. You have
the command in my absence.'

'Yes, *Herr Oberst.*'

Delsingen studied his subordinate closely.
'You don't look very happy, Major.'

'It's not a good idea to take Major
Mindenhof . . .'

'He ought to get out into the field once
in a while. He needs to see there's more to
warfare than parading about in a fancy black
uniform.'

'He's not happy about being hauled into
this, sir.'

'Mindenhof is never happy about anything
unless he's the one initiating it. Hartnitz was
SS. Mindenhof should at least show solidarity,
even if he didn't like the man.'

'Just be very careful out there, sir.'

'I'm taking four men, all Wehrmacht. I don't
think the major will try a field assassination.

By the way, I appreciate your worry, but it is completely unnecessary.'

A sharp knock interrupted them.

'Speaking of the devil,' Delsingen remarked softly. *'Hierein!'*

The door opened and Mindenhof, in full, camouflaged Waffen-SS combat gear and helmet, stomped in. He too carried, in addition to his ever-present pistol, an MP40. He'd also strapped on an ammunition harness to carry six spare magazines. On him, the familiar shape of the helmet looked even more menacing.

The boots clicked, the right hand shot out. *'Heil Hitler!* Reporting for combat duty as ordered, *Herr Oberst!'*

'We're not going into combat, Major,' Delsingen told him mildly, staring at the harness. 'You've got enough magazines to take on a small army. We're simply going to inspect what I believe to be the site of an ambush carried out by Ålvik's people.'

'The terrorists may still be out there.'

'I very much doubt it. It would be stupid of them to remain where they could easily attract an air strike. Not worried, are you?'

'I'm never worried about the enemies of the Reich, Colonel,' Mindenhof snapped.

'Aren't you? I know I am. A man who isn't

worried about his adversaries can make serious tactical errors of judgement.'

Mindenhof's eyes stared lifelessly from beneath the rim of his helmet. 'I am not afraid of a terrorist,' he insisted coldly.

'That's comforting to know.' Delsingen went over to his desk and picked up his helmet and the MP40. 'Come on, Major. The aircraft is waiting. See you by 1500 hours, Geissler,' he added.

'Yes, sir.'

Delsingen put the helmet on as he went out.

Mindenhof gave Geissler an empty stare, before following.

Geissler strode slowly into the outer office, to find the headquarters sergeant peering in the direction Delsingen and Mindenhof had taken.

'Shame about old Hardnuts, sir,' the sergeant began.

' "Hardnuts"?'

'*Leutnant* Hartnitz, sir. For an SS man, he wasn't a bad sort. The men respected him. A tough one, and a real soldier. Not political at all. He used to spend more time with *our* men than with his lot. It's never the shits who go first,' the sergeant finished with sudden vehemence.

Geissler knew he was talking about Mindenhof.

'I didn't hear that, Sergeant,' he remarked sternly.

'No, sir,' the sergeant acknowledged, with due deference to Geissler's rank. 'You didn't.'

'Even if I might have happened to agree.'

'Yes, sir.'

The B138, with an all-Luftwaffe crew, was piloted by a captain. It had landed in the outer harbour, then cruised under its own power to the Vågen, where it now waited. Moored to a floating pier that had been built by Wehrmacht engineers soon after the Occupation had begun, it rode gently on the placid water.

The four-man squad, carrying rifles, marched along the pier, followed by Delsingen and Mindenhof. Two sailors were standing by the mooring lines.

The two officers waited until the men had climbed into the hull of the flying boat, before themselves climbing aboard. The lines were released and a crewman secured the door, then returned to his station.

The triple engines were started. The 138 began to cruise out of Bergen's inner harbour. When it reached open water it increased speed, planed on its stepped hull, then lifted into the air. It banked left to head eastwards, making for the small lake on the Hardangervidda.

Half an hour later, as it was circling low over the lake, the crewman who had secured the door approached Delsingen.

'We have arrived, *Herr Oberst. Hauptmann* Sachsenmüller says he can see bodies.'

Delsingen gave a curt nod, expression neutral. 'Tell him to land, and to try to get us as close to shore as he's able to.'

'Yes, *Herr Oberst.*'

The crewman relayed the message, then once more returned to his station for the landing.

Sachsenmüller carried out a smooth touchdown, then brought the flying boat right up to a part of the shoreline that sloped gently.

'Looks as if you'll be getting your boots wet, Major,' Delsingen said to Mindenhof.

'I'm sure my boots can handle it, Colonel,' Mindenhof responded evenly.

'That was intended as a mild joke,' Delsingen said, then he continued to the soldiers before Mindenhof could say anything further, 'All right, men. As soon as that door opens, I want you out there *fast.*'

'Yes, *Herr Oberst,*' acknowledged the sergeant who led the squad.

The crewman opened the door.

151

'You heard the colonel,' the sergeant barked at his men. '*Move it!*'

They got out swiftly, followed by Delsingen and Mindenhof.

Sachsenmüller had positioned the aircraft perfectly and his passengers had to wade through water that came only halfway up their boots.

As soon as they were clear, two crewmen jumped out and pushed the 138, which moved easily off the shore. They climbed back aboard before it had gone too far.

Sachsenmüller then took it into deeper water, where a sea anchor was deployed to hold it on station. The engines were shut down, bringing a silence so sudden, it sounded deafening.

They found all four bodies.

There was not much left of three of them. Delsingen ordered the sergeant to get them all ready for burial.

He walked some distance away, taking an openly reluctant Mindenhof with him. He stopped to study the area closely, looking at the high rocks from where Ålvik had sprung the devastating ambush. He raised the binoculars to his eyes, searching out the most likely positions for concealment.

'That's the only place they could have been waiting,' he said to Mindenhof. 'It's perfect. Good cover. They must have remained there, waiting for the team to come into range. They used mortars, a sniper and sub-machine-guns.'

'You can tell by just looking around, Colonel?' Mindenhof, looking about him and holding his MP40 ready, clearly did not believe it.

'You saw Hartnitz's body.' Delsingen still held the binoculars to his eyes. 'A single, clean shot. Straight to the heart. The bullet went right through. Hartnitz was dead before he hit the ground. That's the work of a high-powered rifle. The other bodies are either full of holes or shredded. Mortar and machine-gun. Some of these boulders have been shattered. They stood no chance of getting out of the trap, once it had been sprung. This is Ålvik's work. He may even have shadowed them for days.'

'How can you know that?'

Delsingen lowered the binoculars, and turned to the SS major. 'It's what I would have done.'

Mindenhof looked as if he wasn't sure whether to be shocked by the admission, or angered.

'We should make them pay severely for this,'

he said grimly. 'They should be made to learn that an SS officer's life does not come cheaply.' The snout of his MP40 kept tracking round, as if he expected the resistance fighters to appear at any second.

'There are three Wehrmacht bodies here as well,' Delsingen reminded him gently.

'Of course, Colonel. I meant the life of any German.'

'Of course.'

'We should take severe reprisals,' Mindenhof insisted.

'Reprisals. They won't do much good.' Delsingen glanced down at Mindenhof's MP40. 'That won't be of much use, either, if a sniper's still out there.'

The MP40 abruptly stopped moving with a sharp jerk, as if the barrel had been slammed against an invisible wall.

'Relax, Major,' Delsingen said drily. 'If there had been a sniper around, we would all have been dead by now. Or at least some of us would have been. I've seen enough. Time to get back.'

He began walking back to where the squad, with tools from the aircraft, were preparing to bury the dead.

After a moment's hesitation a tight-lipped Mindenhof followed him.

The burial was completed without drama. As they stood silently over the graves, it was as if there were no other people in the world, so still did the very air about them feel.

The two officers saluted the rough mounds. Even here, Mindenhof gave the outstretched arm salute.

Each grave was marked at the head by the combat knife that had belonged to each soldier, and which had been thrust into the earth to the hilt.

They were making their way back to the shore of the lake, when Mindenhof said, 'We should have taken them back. They should not have been left here, in this empty place.'

'Before this war is over, Major,' Delsingen began evenly, 'many Germans will be without any graves at all, in places much further away from Germany than here.'

Being some distance from the soldiers, they could not be overheard.

'Those sound like words of defeat,' Mindenhof said.

'No, Major. Words of reality. People die in war, and, believe it or not, even conquerors.'

'Sometimes,' Delsingen said, after he'd told Geissler of the events by the lake, 'I despair of that man, even beyond what I expect of him.'

Once again in standard uniform, he leaned back in his chair with a sigh.

Geissler cast a quick glance at the map. 'As there was no hostile contact up there, Colonel, where do you think Ålvik will strike next?'

'Your guess is as good as mine. However, the more teams we have out in the field, the less room he is going to have for manoeuvre. We'll eliminate his people by attrition, while keeping our own casualties down. He was very lucky to catch Hartnitz the way he did. We all need luck sometimes. But sooner or later, he'll put in an appearance where we'll be waiting for him. Then we'll have him.

'You know, Geissler, one has to admire the man. He will not give up. I wonder if we shall be as good when our turn comes.'

'You expect us to be fighting on the roads and streets of Germany?'

'It's the natural consequence of things, Major.'

'But Barbarossa is doing well. The Luftwaffe destroyed nearly two thousand Russian aircraft on the first day.'

'On 22 June,' Delsingen said thoughtfully. 'I wonder what future historians will make of that date. We are only in September. There's plenty of time for things to go wrong.' Delsingen got to his feet and went over to the map. He stared at it for long seconds. 'And they will.'

Kearns and Bede were again over the Channel, forty-five minutes into their patrol.

The two Spitfires sped low over a surface that was choppy enough to display white horses. As usual, Bede was keeping perfect formation on his leader. He searched the tufted patchwork of clouds above him for enemy aircraft. Nothing flitted between them.

Then, seconds later, he spotted two shapes, ahead and above. Big enough at that distance to be bombers. He glanced across at Kearns.

Kearns had also seen the enemy bombers and, catching Bede's glance, nodded to show he was aware of them. Checking for fighters and spotting none in the immediate vicinity, he opened the throttle and gave chase, staying low.

Bede was right there with him, already understanding how the attack was going to develop. They now worked so well together that Kearns felt it was as if their nerve ends were linked together. Bede always seemed to know what was needed of him.

They began to gain on the bombers, which

turned out to be two Ju-88s. Despite the fact that Spitfires lost some performance at such low level, Kearns chose not to gain altitude. He continued the pursuit, inexorably drawing closer to the bombers. He also made a periodic check of the sky above, just in case any fighters made an appearance. So far, none had. The thing to hope for was that the bombers would not spot them before they were close enough to attack, and so have enough time to call in either any high-flying escorts that might be lurking upstairs or any free-ranging fighters in the vicinity.

Kearns reasoned that the bomber crews would be keeping a primary lookout above, as their own altitude, though greater than that of the closing Spitfires, was still low enough for them to expect an attack from a higher level.

He glanced at Bede's aircraft. His wingman was right there, holding his usual perfect station as the choppy waters rushed past beneath them.

They had got closer still and yet there continued to be no evidence of alarm from the enemy bombers. The gunner in the ventral gondola beneath the cockpit, with its rearwards-facing twin guns, must be asleep, he reasoned. So much the better. He'd soon be waking up, just in time for a more permanent slumber.

The 1440hp Merlin 45 roared exultantly as the range closed.

Please don't jam, Kearns prayed over and over in his mind to the guns.

He eased the rudder slightly to the left to get into position for the left-hand target. As if in seamless choreography, he saw Bede's aircraft shift slightly to the right, taking up position for an attack on the second aircraft.

Yet still the gunners on both Ju-88s appeared not to notice anything.

Kearns then came to the conclusion that their approach, so close to the water, must somehow be managing to keep them undetectable. All that would change once they began to rise for the shark-like attack. They would be discovered and three things would immediately occur: the gunners would fire; their warning to their pilots would cause the bombers to take immediate evasive action; and they would call out the fighters.

'We must get them before any of these things happens,' Kearns muttered to himself.

Or at least in time to make any of the above actions purely academic.

It was time.

Kearns gently pulled the stick back. The rushing Spitfire went into a high-speed, shallow climb.

Bede was following suit, as if tied to Kearns's Spitfire.

Then the gunners woke up.

But it was already too late. Even as the tracers began reaching out for him and the bomber seemed to have suddenly become large, Kearns was squeezing the button on the spade grip of the control stick.

The guns did not let him down. The six weapons hurled their combined fire-power of cannon shell and bullets in a ferocious, two-second barrage at the Ju-88. Forty 20mm shells and 133 machine-gun rounds, a combined weight of 25lb, slammed with terrific force into the gondola, chewing its way through to rage into the cockpit above, killing both the gunner and the pilot. It was enough.

Kearns had to yank the Spitfire into a hard left-hand avoidance turn as the bomber suddenly tipped over and headed downwards. By the time he'd rolled upright again and was into the climb, the Ju-88 was plunging steeply. Even if someone else had been able to get at the controls, there was not enough time for a pull-out. The aircraft slammed into the sea, spreading a great circle of foaming water.

Kearns looked round for Bede. He need not have worried. A bright Roman candle of flame gave him the answer as the second bomber plunged in a terminal dive.

'That boy *is* good,' Kearns said to himself.

'*Fighters!*' he heard suddenly. 'Downhill! Six o'clock!'

So the bombers had found time to raise the alarm.

He checked out Bede's warning call. And there they were: two rapidly expanding dots hurtling towards them.

The Spitfire had not yet lost appreciable speed in the climb and he curved round for a head-on pass. He saw that Bede had done the same.

The two enemy fighters turned out to be Messerschmitt 109s.

Either because their diving speed was already too great for ease of manoeuvring, or their pilots had misinterpreted the Spitfires' own manoeuvre, they went right past the climbing RAF fighters without firing a single shot.

'What the hell . . . ?' Kearns muttered. He rolled the Spitfire on to its back and went back down.

The 109 had a neat trick. Because of its

injected engine, the pilot could push the stick forward and go into a high-speed dive, streaking away from a pursuing Spitfire. In the Spitfire's case, its carburetted engine prevented it from doing likewise, as the negative Gs would starve the engine of much-needed fuel, causing it to cut out. There could be worse ways of losing the fight in air combat than with a faltering engine, but caught in such a situation not many pilots would think so if the adversary was concentrating on putting as many holes into you as he could in the shortest possible time.

Before the Spitfire could dive with its engine on full song, it was necessary to first roll inverted to keep positive G on the carburettors, and pull into the dive, before rolling upright again. The problem with that was that it took enough time to allow the quarry to scoot away as he went downhill.

Kearns, however, preferred the Spitfire way. He also had a method of slicing into the turn, shaving fractions off the time it took to complete the manoeuvre. He hated negative gravity, which was what happened when the stick was pushed forward in such a move. The pilot would be forced off his seat and into his harness, with the blood trying its best to send a tidal wave into his brain, giving him 'red-out'. Kearns called the condition the 'morning-after-a-bad-booze-night', because of the bloodshot eyes the phenomenon tended to induce.

As the Spitfire flipped on to its back, Kearns looked up through the inverted canopy and spotted a 109 far below. He pulled into the dive, rolled upright and hurtled towards the enemy fighter. As he fell towards the water, it occurred to him that something relatively simple may have happened to create the present situation.

'The bastards misjudged it!' he said to himself in happy surprise.

It happened. One moment you thought you had all options covered, then you made a silly mistake. If he was right, both the 109 pilots had grossly miscalculated and would try to recover the initiative. On such small things could the tide of a battle turn.

'Better you than me,' he grunted as he closed rapidly on the 109.

Then he realized why the closure rate was so high. The Messerschmitt was pulling out of the dive. Its speed had been so great that its initial recovery was slow as the pilot hauled on the stick, straining against the punishing G forces.

Kearns throttled back and began to ease the stick towards him, bringing the nose up early. By doing this, he was matching his momentum to that of the 109 and was keeping the gunsight positioned on a spot just behind the 109's birdcage cockpit.

But he was not close enough.

He kept falling upon the German fighter, continuously flattening the dive as the target aircraft began to curve upwards. Kearns knew that if the enemy pilot looked behind him at any moment, he would spot the descending Spitfire and roll out of the way. Kearns wanted him to keep concentrating on pulling out for just a while longer.

He drew closer. The black crosses were well within the sights now. Closer still.

'Easy, easy,' Kearns said to himself softly. 'Don't rush it.' Please, guns, he added mentally. Don't let me down.

They didn't.

When he fired, they roared out a song of fiendish glee. Twenty-five pounds of hellish metal tore into the Messerschmitt, ripping the entire tail completely off. Thus destabilized, the remainder of the aircraft gyrated wildly in response to the powerful torque of its still-racing engine.

Kearns stared wide-eyed as the canopy flew off and the pilot was sucked out of the cockpit. The parachute didn't open.

He banked away, looking for Bede.

A silent explosion in a relatively cloudless part of the sky caught his attention. He saw with relief that it wasn't Bede because not far from the scene a Spitfire was performing an exuberant roll. It could only be the irrepressible Bede.

Kearns did a quick scan of the air about him. You never knew who could be waiting ready to pounce on a pilot enjoying his victory. But no enemy fighters were in sight.

Bede rejoined formation and they continued the patrol, completing it without further combat.

When they landed, the mechanic who had once spoken to Kearns's aircraft came up to them.

'Any trouble with the guns today, sir?'

'None,' Kearns said. 'She's really behaving herself. I've seen you speak to her once or twice, just before I taxi. What do you say?'

'I tell her she'd better fire those guns or I'll cut her up for scrap.'

'You *what?*' Kearns stared at the mechanic as if the man had taken leave of his senses. 'Are you pulling my leg? You're talking as if she could hear you.'

'Your guns worked, didn't they, sir? Who knows with these things.'

'Well,' Kearns said after some moments, 'keep talking to her.'

The mechanic grinned. 'If you say so, sir.'

'I do say so.'

As they walked away from their aircraft, Bede said, 'You don't really believe that, do you, Jo-Jo? An *aircraft* being scared of being turned into scrap? That's a line.'

'The guns worked, didn't they?'

7

September 1943
Flight Lieutenant (Acting Squadron Leader) John Kearns, DSO, DFC, was no longer at his original station. His squadron had been posted to East Anglia for the past year. But he still flew his original Spitfire Vb, and it continued to look after him. He had never been shot down, and the aircraft continued to go serenely through the war without a scratch. Jo-Jo's luck had become the stuff of legend.

A peculiar thing had occurred on the day before the squadron was due to move. The mechanic who used to look after the aircraft was killed when the truck in which he was a passenger skidded on a wet road and careered into a ditch. The skid had been relatively mild, and the ditch shallow. But it was not the skid that had killed him. The incident had taken place at night, in rain. The mechanic had climbed unhurt up to the side of the road, to flag down some help – and was hit by another truck.

Kearns had enjoyed an unbroken spell of jam-free guns. The very next day, while on patrol, he had closed in nicely on a Focke-Wulf 190. The guns had refused to fire.

In desperation after landing, he had yelled the mechanic's threat at the aircraft.

The guns had once again begun to work properly. He made no attempt to explain the phenomenon to himself. The guns worked when he needed them, and that was that.

Many of the old faces had gone. The remaining two of the three young pilots who had been commenting about his luck were all gone. Shot down. James Bede had been posted to the desert theatre, where he had continued his single-minded determination to shoot down as many aircraft as he possibly could. He was now a flight lieutenant, DSO and Bar, DFC and Bar, with twenty victories. He had been shot down twice, but had only once been slightly wounded. He complained bitterly at the time it was because he was no longer flying on Kearns's wing that he kept getting shot down.

As a flight commander, Kearns now had an office of sorts, in a Nissen hut. He was staring out of a window at a particularly bleak Norfolk day, bleak in mood himself, when there was a knock on the door. The squadron commander entered.

Squadron Leader Harry Luwzinsky's Polish father had come to Britain just before the First World War, only to die in it after volunteering, in 1915. He never saw his son.

Luwzinsky, a veteran of several missions and survivor of a Spitfire crash, had an unmarked face; but his body was a mass of scars as a result of the crash, when his disintegrating aircraft appeared to have flung most of itself at him. It was still a wonder to many that he had not broken a single bone.

A short, stocky man with a severe, short-back-and-sides haircut and deep-grey eyes, he always seemed full of humour. It was hard to equate him with the person who so ruthlessly tore into the enemy in the air at every opportunity. He was also an excellent commander. He had been shot down five times – on one occasion twice in the same day – but never wounded.

'Well, Jo-Jo,' he said to Kearns. 'Sad day.'

'Yes, sir. I'll hate leaving my old kite.'

'She's served you well. Perhaps she'll look after whoever takes her over from now on.'

'I'll really miss her.'

'Cheer up, old chap. You're getting a fabulous, brand-new Mossie.'

'And an extra crew member. I'm a single-seater man.'

'The powers that be obviously think otherwise. They've got plans for you.'

'What do they know?' Kearns was not to be comforted.

'I dare say we'll soon find out. After all, I'm going too. At least, it won't be all strangers.'

'But *Scotland*! My God, sir. What's it going to be like up there in the winter? I come from Queensland. I hate winters.'

'You'll cope,' Luwzinsky said cheerfully. 'This news might brighten your day. You're going to be the deputy CO.'

Kearns stared at Luwzinsky. 'You're joking . . . er, sir.'

'No joke. You're my number two. So you see? The brass do know something, after all. They can spot a good man at fifty paces . . . when they're looking.' He grinned, seeming unexpectedly boyish. 'We'll be doing our conversion training in Sussex, then fly our aircraft up to the new posting.'

'Any idea as yet what the posting's about.'

The squadron leader shook his head. 'All I can tell you is that this is a new squadron being formed from scratch, for a specific task. I've no idea what that task is supposed to be. Well, I'd better be getting on. Got to hand over to the new chap who's replacing me. Just popped in to see how you were doing, and to give you the glad news.'

'I've already handed over to Jock Peebles.'

'Good show. See you in the mess later?'

'Yes, sir.'

Luwzinsky peered out at the weather. 'Nasty stuff. Hope the Yanks are not sending their bombers out in this. Took a terrible pasting last month on that Schweinfurt raid, poor blighters. Who'd fly a bomber, no matter how well armed?'

'Someone has to do it, I suppose.'

'Yes. Lucky we don't. See you later.'

Kearns nodded. 'Yes, sir.'

He turned once more, to look out at the bleak day. Deputy squadron commander.

Now there was something.

In Bergen, Delsingen, now a senior colonel, was still in command of *Sondergruppe-Norwegen*, which had proved to be extremely successful at suppressing the resistance. The teams had gained fresh impetus from the deaths of Hartnitz and his men. For a period immediately following

the incident, they had scored several successes.
A team led by Geissler had wiped out a group
as far away as Ålesund. What was more, many
of these defeated resistance fighters had turned
out to be from Ålvik's group. But Ålvik himself
had never been caught; nor had those closest
to him.

Resistance in the area, however, had virtually
disappeared. There were still sporadic attacks,
but these had now become so few and far
between that Delsingen believed only one small
group was still operating.

But the tide of war was changing for the
Reich, and not for the better. To begin with,
the promised expansion of the *Sondergruppe*
idea had not come. All efforts were now
being concentrated on making the Sognefjord,
proposed lair of the *Graf von Hiller*, a virtual
fortress. As far as the Führer was concerned,
the war was far from lost. It would go on. As
Delsingen had long thought bitterly, until the
eventual destruction of Germany. Like many
others, he had seen it coming.

But we did nothing, he reminded himself.
And we'll pay for that.

Von Arnim had surrendered earlier in the
year in North Africa. Now Montgomery and
the Americans were pounding up from Italy.

The Russians were rolling back Barbarossa. Bomber raids were frequent over the Fatherland, despite the severe punishment they took from the Luftwaffe. The enemy could take the punishment and still come back with even more aircraft. The Luftwaffe could not. Inevitably, the constant attrition would whittle the fighters and their pilots down to the point where the skies over Germany would belong to the Allies.

'And even up here in Norway,' he said to himself, 'the enemy's aircraft have been increasingly active.'

Mindenhof had got his promotion to *Obersturmbannführer* and had become even more insufferable. From his point of view, the war was still being won.

A knock interrupted Delsingen's reverie and Geissler entered, carrying a folder.

The Wehrmacht major had been decorated with the Iron Cross, First Class, for extreme bravery under fire. During a fight in which his team had been facing far superior numbers, he had held on for three days in a running battle towards a rendezvous point, losing just one man. The route to the rendezvous had been strewn with the bodies of his pursuers.

Geissler had changed. His eyes held secrets he hated. The news of what had been really going on in the concentration camps could no longer be ignored. He had met a wounded veteran from the Eastern Front in a local hospital when on one of his rare visits to his parents, and what the man had said to him had sickened him. If only half of what that veteran had told him were true, it would still be a terrible curse upon the name of Germany that would last for generations. He had seen the devastation wrought by Allied bombing and fully understood that the reckoning was only a matter of time. And in his heart was the shaming weight of the love he had betrayed.

Was she, he asked himself continually, even now dying in a camp somewhere? Was she long dead?

'Well, Geissler,' Delsingen was saying. 'The whirlwind is coming.'

'Don't let Mindenhof hear you, sir. He still believes we're winning.'

'Yes, I know. Now that he's a lieutenant colonel it will become more difficult to keep him in check. The SS are already blaming the Wehrmacht for every defeat. He sees his star in the ascendant.'

'You still have your *Gruppenführer* friend.'

'*Obergruppenführer* now. See, Geissler? The SS are getting all the promotions.'

'At least, that's a good thing for you. *He* will hold Mindenhof in check.'

'Perhaps,' Delsingen said philosophically. 'Mindenhof sees me as the epitome of all he hates about the Wehrmacht. According to him, we have betrayed the Reich. Goering blamed the Luftwaffe for not beating the British, back in 1940. Now people like Mindenhof blame the Wehrmacht for what is happening on the ground. He's been waiting a long time for my head. The time of the scapegoat is upon us, and it will get worse as the war continues. But I've got bad news for our SS lieutenant colonel. He won't get my head. Now what's that you've brought?'

Geissler passed the folder to Delsingen. 'Coded, urgent priority. I decoded it myself. No one else has seen it.'

'You don't look very happy, Ernst.'

'Read it first, sir.'

'That bad, is it?'

Delsingen slowly opened the folder. A sealed envelope was on top of the decoded message. The SS seal on the envelope was a clear indication of its origin. He read the message first. Twice.

'So,' he said quietly. 'It would appear that the *Graf von Hiller* is nearly complete, and

175

the Allies still have no idea of its existence.
It's expected in Norway early next year and
our job is to provide anti-aircraft protection.
We're to leave Mindenhof in charge of security.'
Delsingen passed a hand over his eyes. 'God help
us, and God help the local people. The worse the
war gets for us, the more excesses he will
commit. I must stop this.'

He picked up the sealed letter and opened
it. It read:

Rüdi,
    I know this will come as a shock to you,
but you are now a brigadier general! The
documentation will come via the usual
channels. You may not like the new
appointment, but look at it this way.
You are not being sent into harm's way,
but being taken out of it. If you think a
while on this, you will understand. Take
what personnel you wish, to establish
your new headquarters. You will still
have a certain degree of autonomy. In
other words, you can still keep a check
on the security arrangements for the area.
As usual, I will back you if you need to
rap a few knuckles.'
    Max

Delsingen folded the letter slowly. 'It seems as if I may have been wrong about the SS and their promotions.'

Geissler waited.

'I seem to have been made a brigadier general, Ernst.'

Geissler's face creased into a huge grin. 'Congratulations, General!' He held out his hand. 'This will kill Mindenhof.'

The newly promoted General Delsingen shook the hand. 'Thank you, Ernst. As you will have seen by that signal, we have a new posting.'

' "We", sir?'

'We.' Delsingen tapped at the letter. 'According to this, I have the authority to set up my new headquarters with whatever staff I require. I can't have a major as my number two. I need a lieutenant colonel. At the very least.'

'I understand, sir.'

'No you don't, Lieutenant Colonel Geissler.'

Geissler's eyes widened. '*Me?*'

'Is there another Geissler in this room?'

'Er, no, sir.'

'Good. I can't think of anyone else better suited. By the time we have set up the new HQ, your file will have been amended accordingly and the promotion officially sanctioned. In the

meantime, we had better get to work. There's
plenty to do.'

'Yes, sir! And what about Mindenhof?'

Delsingen gave a tight smile. 'I'll still be able
to keep a check on him.' He tapped the letter
again. 'The *Obergruppenführer* says so.'

Geissler still had the grin pasted on his face.
'This will really kill Mindenhof.'

'It will also make him more dangerous. I
think my friend,' Delsingen continued, 'wanted
me away from here, to prevent Mindenhof from
yielding to temptation.'

'What temptation?'

'To put a bullet in me, of course.'

Geissler has been quite correct about Mindenhof's
possible reaction to the news of the promotions.

The SS lieutenant colonel had come to
Delsingen's office, still unaware of the double upgrading, but eager to assert his newly
established authority. The shock was yet
to come.

He had stomped into the office, barked his
usual '*Heil Hitler*', and was standing glower-
ing at Delsingen. Geissler stood in a corner,
watching in anticipation.

'I have a copy of the signal,' Mindenhof
began. 'I am now in command here.'

'Not just yet, Colonel . . .'

'*Obersturmbannführer!* Address me by my correct rank!'

'Not just yet, Colonel,' Delsingen repeated calmly. 'You're not quite in command. And I ought to remind you that you really should observe protocol when addressing an officer of general rank.'

The dark eyes seemed to pop. '*What?*' Mindenhof demanded weakly, the chagrin plain on his face. 'You have been promoted to general?' He could not have helped himself.

' "Sir", Colonel. Promoted to general, "sir".'

Mindenhof swallowed. 'Sir,' he got out at last, nearly choking on the word.

'Yes, Colonel. Amazing, isn't it? And Geissler is now a lieutenant colonel. Just like you, in fact.'

Mindenhof's head snapped round to look at Geissler, eyes venomous. 'A lieutenant colonel,' he said tightly.

Geissler smiled thinly at him.

Mindenhof jerked his head round again to look at Delsingen. 'When do I take command . . . sir?'

'When I tell you. We have plenty of work to do, so let's all get on with it. And Colonel, what I said long ago still stands. You will not

abuse the locals. I'll still be able to check
on you.'

Mindenhof's eyes gave one of their more
malevolent dances. He took a deep breath.
His right arm shot out.

'*Heil Hitler!*' he snarled, wheeled and stomped
out.

'There goes a very desperate man, Geissler,'
Delsingen said when Mindenhof had gone. 'He
would burn the whole of Norway if he thought
he could get away with it.'

'Perhaps there might come a time when even
that might not restrain him.'

'Let us hope the war will be over before he
reaches that stage,' Delsingen said.

Whitehall, London

Delsingen had been wrong when he'd said that
the Allies did not know of the existence of the
Graf von Hiller; but the knowledge had come
almost perilously close to being too late.

The shabby-suited men were still in their
job, in their shabby office, but now they had
been galvanized by more information that had
recently come to them about the ship. As a result,
they had begun to cross-refer to the first snippets
of information they had received so long ago.

They had stared, shocked, at both the

supposed specifications of the ship and the purpose for which it had been constructed. In trying to make up for their earlier mistake, they were commendably swift in initiating the kind of action that would subsequently cause the paths of Jo-Jo Kearns and General Delsingen to cross in conflict. Per Ålvik and Delsingen would also cross paths, but not in the way either might have expected.

The men were now studying the latest information that had come in. The ship was still being deployed to Norway, but there was no indication of when. A high-flying photo-recce Spitfire had been sent to take pictures, and though a veritable swarm of fighters had risen to meet it, they had not been able to catch the unarmed PR aircraft. However, the pictures it had taken had been of the wrong location. It was obvious that many dummy ships had been built, and costly bombing raids to try to destroy the real one had been suspended after three dummies had been hit.

A different strategy had thus been planned. It had been decided to wait until the ship had actually been deployed and then to destroy it in its Norwegian lair.

The latest information indicated that deployment was now imminent.

Sussex, England

The Spitfire Vb came sweeping low over the airfield at Merston, in weather than was far better than in Norfolk. It banked steeply, wingtip seeming almost to touch the ground as it performed two complete rolls, then rose in a flashing climb. It pulled into a half loop, flew upside down, then squared the loop by pulling into the dive once more. As it dropped, it began to level out, slowing down as it did so. It arrived over the threshold at the right speed and height for a smooth touchdown.

'One day,' said someone watching, 'he's going to misjudge that.'

'Crazy Norwegian,' another commented pleasantly. 'Got another two today, by the looks.'

When he'd taxied to the flight line and had come to a stop, the pilot found the squadron CO waiting for him.

'Flight Lieutenant Ålvik,' the CO began as Ålvik climbed down from the aircraft.

'Sir?'

'Don't look so worried, man. I'm not going

to bawl you out for that ridiculous display . . . even if it's quite, er, impressive.'

'Yes . . . no, sir.'

'Quit while you're head, Ålvik.' The CO was Canadian.

'Yes, sir.'

'Right, Mr Ålvik, it seems some high-up people require your services . . .'

'I'm *leaving*? I don't want to . . .'

'Don't interrupt me again, Flight Lieutenant.'

'No, sir!'

'All right. You've been asked for, and I've got to let you go. I've no choice in the matter. Your immediate posting is not far from here. You'll be converting to a new aircraft. Whatever it is they want you to do, don't let the squadron down.'

'I won't, sir.'

'That's the stuff, Mr Ålvik. Now I guess you'd better check with the Movements people.'

'Yes, sir.'

The CO saluted. 'Good luck, Mr Ålvik.'

'Thank you, sir.'

Two weeks later, after some leave, Luwzinsky and Kearns arrived at their new unit. Some of the people who were to crew the Mosquitoes were already there. Others had still to arrive.

The incredible de Havilland Mosquito was an aircraft that was a departure from standard aircraft construction. From the outset in 1938, it was planned to be constructed in wood, with the added bonus that it would ease the demand on metals much needed for other wartime construction. The twin-engined aircraft had turned out to be even better than its designers had dared hope. Built in an astonishing number of variants, those allocated to Kearns's new unit came in three marks.

The F Mk 2 was essentially the fighter version, with an armament of four .303 Browning machine-guns and four 20mm Hispano cannon. The FB Mk 6 was classed as a fighter-bomber and based on the Mk 2. Specifically for intruder missions, it carried the same armament as the fighter version, but could also carry bombs either within its bomb bay or externally; or eight 60lb rockets – four under each wing.

The third variant was a monster. This was the FB Mk XVIII. The 'Eighteen', as some of the unit's crews would call it, or the Tse-Tse Fly, as it was more commonly known, had a good reason for the nickname. The four-cannon fit in its shark-like jaw beneath the cockpit had been replaced by a single, awesome cannon, a 57mm six-pounder Molins gun. This was the Tse-Tse's true proboscis. It was a tank gun and, on the Mosquito, was a terrifying weapon. Like its African namesake, it brought with it an explosive and permanent sleeping sickness. This double-identity, Merlin-engined 'insect' could also be fully tooled up with the additional eight rocket projectiles, or externally carried bombs. The four .303 Brownings in the nose were retained.

These were the aircraft that greeted Kearns on his arrival. There were eighteen in all, six of each variant.

'Well,' he said to Luwzinsky, 'they're a bit bigger than the Spit.'

'And you've got two lovely Merlins instead of one.'

'Even so.'

'There's no satisfying some people,' Luwzinsky remarked drily. 'This is the Wooden Wonder. Come on. Let's report to the Station Commander.'

'Before going to the mess?'

'Before the mess.'

'Welcome, gentlemen,' the group captain greeted them. A wing commander navigator with a chestful of ribbons and a thin moustache was with him. 'This is Wing Commander Smythe. The wing commander has some information to which you should listen very closely. Wing Commander, if you please.'

'Sir.'

Smythe, a man of average height, had sleek black hair parted in the middle. His eyes glowed the deepest blue that Kearns had ever seen. The Australian thought he looked like a matinée idol and half expected to see a long, white silk scarf hanging from his neck. The decorations beneath the navigator's half-wing proved that film-star looks or not, this man was no pampered softie in combat.

'We are forming this unit for a specific purpose,' Smythe began. 'To eliminate a battleship.' He looked at each face as he said that. 'I can see by your expressions you may be going into an advanced state of shock. I'm afraid you heard me correctly. The ship in question, a pocket battleship to rival all the other heavy German ships, is called the *Graf von Hiller*, and she outperforms – according to her specifications – everything else afloat – on either side.

'We know she has not yet been deployed, but she soon will be. This means she has not yet had her shake-down cruise. Her intended safe haven is to be the Sognefjord. This is Norway's biggest fiord. It is longer and deeper than any of the others. The vital statistics are these: 127 miles long and nearly 4,300 feet deep. That's deeper than the North Sea.

'This great depth means the *von Hiller* might well be at sea herself, for all the worries her captain will have about grounding. It also means we can't hope to force her aground, unless she can be made to try to run for it, going too close to the shore and doing so too fast for the narrower sections of the fiord or the many islands and skerries which abound. The risk in that option, of course, is that she might well manage to escape into the open sea. We can't have that. We expect her to berth as far in as possible, as a precaution against air attack. This will give us a very deep gauntlet to run to reach the target. However, once she's disabled in there, she's trapped.

'Her armaments comprise six fifteen-inch guns; fourteen 5.9-inch; sixteen 105mm cannon, sixteen 37mm, thirty-six 20mm; and a further twelve Oerlikon. No surface ship will get within sufficient range to do any damage, without being blown out of the water first. An air attack with fast, light bombers is the only feasible answer. B-17s or Lancs, equally, would be blown out of the sky before they could get close enough to drop their bombs. Within the confines of the fiord, they would be totally unable to manoeuvre without either hitting each other or flying into a cliff face. They would also be sitting ducks for the AA barrage that would be coming up at them.

'We can expect a standing fighter cover, as well as anti-aircraft defences all the way in, and back again. Without doubt, there'll be other surface ships in the fiord, to act as a further defensive screen. You can count on their putting up a fierce AA barrage of their own.

'Given the depth of the fiord, it was originally planned to use submarines. However, it is assumed that in addition to the surface ship defences, which would include destroyers and other depth-charge-wielding vessels, there will also be a virtually impregnable anti-submarine net system and, quite possibly, a series of nets and booms, protecting the ship.

'This armoured raider is very important to the Germans. Destroying it will be a tremendous blow to their morale. The effects of this blow will permeate down to the lowliest soldier. It could mean the difference between a wavering motivation, if we succeed, and a resolute one, if that ship escapes.

'One of our pilots is Norwegian, with a comprehensive local knowledge. He will be able to help us devise the best way to plan our attack. It is intended to attack this ship *before* she has had a chance to work up to full operational capability and while her crew is still getting to know their ship and each other. This lack of familiarity with the ship, its systems and among the crew, will lengthen their response time to attack. It may be the only leeway we have.

'It is believed that her primary task will be to hunt down all shipping within our waters. This gives her a fairly large hunting ground and plenty of room within which to "disappear", until the next attack. I am giving no secrets away when I tell you that the invasion of Europe will come eventually. Even Hitler realizes this. Therefore this *Überschiff* of his must *not* be allowed to run amok among our own shipping lanes.

'If she is as good as she threatens to be, it is not difficult to understand why the Germans planned her construction so long ago, and in such secrecy. Her formidable array of weaponry can help delay the outcome of the war, perhaps long enough to enable Hitler to recoup his losses. This could have disastrous implications. Our task, gentlemen, is a difficult one; but it is one that we must carry out. In the Mosquito, we have at our disposal the tool with which to do the job.' Smythe stopped at last. 'Questions?'

Kearns looked at the wing commander. 'Yes, sir. The bloke who planned this, is he all right in the head?'

Luwzinsky gave Kearns a startled look. The group captain's expression froze. Smythe actually smiled.

'I thought the same thing,' he replied.

'Then you can tell him from me, sir, he's nuts.'

'I'm certain he'll be interested to hear that. I'll tell him exactly what you have said.'

The group captain now had a strange expression on his face.

'The question is,' Smythe was saying, 'can it be done?'

'Anything can be attempted, sir,' Kearns said. 'It's a matter of whether or not you survive, or whether or not you get the job done. From what you've just said, neither seems possible. No survival, no target blitzed. Zero. No go.'

'So what do you suggest we do about that ship, Squadron Leader . . .'

The deep-blue eyes remained fastened on the Australian. Smythe said nothing, and seemed to be waiting.

'The way I see it,' Kearns continued, unde-
terred, 'we haven't much of a choice. We can't
let that ship go. Which means I'm as crazy as
the bloke who planned this. But we should try
to make the odds more even.'

'That's why you're here, and all the others
who are coming. To even the odds. That is
why we've been given the Mossie. Again, to
even the odds. The enemy is already so scared
of that aircraft, the mere sight of it worries
him intensely. We have picked the best crews
for the job. Everyone who's not already here
will be by tomorrow. Training begins the day
after. You and your second in command might
as well start getting to know your personnel,
Wing Commander Luwzinsky.'

'*Wing commander*, sir?' Luwzinsky asked.

'Yes. And your promotion to Squadron
Leader is confirmed, Kearns.' Smythe turned
to the group captain. 'Isn't that right, sir?'

The group captain nodded. 'It is.'

'And Kearns . . . Smythe went on.

'Sir?'

'As one crazy person to another . . .'

Kearns stared at him. '*Your* plan?'

'My plan.'

Kearns was silent for some moments. 'Then
we had better make it work.'

'I agree.'

A roar of Merlins swept over the building as a pair of Spitfires took to the air.

Kearns found a pleasant surprise waiting for him in the mess.

'Any guns jammed lately?' a voice said behind him.

Kearns whirled. 'Well, well. I'll be . . . You old wombat. Where did you spring from?'

Bede was grinning at him, hand outstretched. They shook hands enthusiastically.

'Jerry moved out of Africa,' Bede said. 'Things got boring. I got fed up of wearing khaki, so when the buzz came about selection for a new unit, I put my name up. Then I heard you were deputy CO. I couldn't believe it. Just like old times, I thought. It also means I can stop getting shot down, now that we're on the same team again.'

Kearns looked at the ribbons on Bede's tunic. 'Having a good war, I see, Flight Lieutenant.'

Bede pointed to Kearns's own ribbons. 'So are you, Squadron Leader.'

'You know how it is. They throw these things away. Ranks, gongs . . .'

Bede grinned once more. 'Who would have thought we'd have wound up on Mossies?

Remember the one that flew over our old squadron?'

'I do.'

'Must have been an omen of some kind,' Bede said. 'So,' he continued eagerly. 'What's the story?'

'That, my dear Venerable, will make your toes curl.'

'They're curling already. A tough one, is it?'

'Very.'

'Should I un-volunteer?'

'It might be smart.'

'Ah well. Too late. I've had a chat with some of the boys,' Bede went on. 'All sorts of bods. Looks like we've got ourselves an international squadron. One's a Norwegian. Do you know he used to be in the resistance over there? Came over about a year or so ago, learned to fly and turned into a raging fighter pilot.'

'Where is he? We had a briefing about him. Assuming he's the same one.

'He's the only Norwegian, so he must be. See the serious-looking chap over there with the coffee? That's him. Although he hasn't been in the Norwegian air force,' Bede continued, propelling Kearns by the arm towards Ålvik, 'he apparently had some kind of civilian student licence. Anyway, he got through his flying training in record time and found himself on Spits. Interesting chap. Killed lots of Germans even before he got over here. Seems he's just continuing what he began.'

They had reached Ålvik.

'Per,' Bede said, 'Jo-Jo Kearns, deputy CO. He's a lucky man. Never been shot down. When we flew together I was never shot down either. Then I was posted, and got shot down twice. I'm glad to be here.'

Ålvik had come to attention. 'Flight Lieutenant Ålvik, sir.'

'At ease, Per,' Kearns said. 'Besides, standing to attention with a hot coffee in your hand looks a bit dangerous.' He smiled at the Norwegian.

Ålvik's own smile was hesitant, his eyes guarded.

'I hear you're quite familiar with where we're supposed to be going,' Kearns said to him.

Ålvik nodded, but said nothing.

'Then we'll be wanting to talk to you in detail at some stage,' Kearns said, watching the other closely. 'And if there's anything else you'd like to talk to me about . . . privately, feel free to do so.'

'I will,' Ålvik said. 'Thank you, sir.'

'Good-oh.'

As they walked on, Bede said, 'What was that about? Why would he want to talk to you privately?'

'There's something on his mind.'

'Really? I hadn't noticed . . .'

'The trouble with you, James, is that you think only of killing the Hun.'

'Is that such a bad thing?'

'No.'

8

The next day Smythe held the first formal briefing for the entire squadron. He did not tell them the identity of the intended target, but impressed on them the need for the intense conversion to the new aircraft. The real operational training would take place after all crews had successfully completed the conversion course.

Many pilots had come from single-seaters, but there were former heavy- and medium-bomber crews too. For the eighteen aircraft, a pool of thirty crews was available. It was expected that the failure rate and attrition due to accidents would bring that reserve down.

The three different marks of aircraft had specific roles and the crews to man them were chosen accordingly. The single-seater pilots were given the Mk 2, the bomber crews got the Mk 6, and a mixture of fighter and fighter-bomber pilots got the Tse-Tse 'Eighteen'. Their navigators, like those on the Mk 2, came from the 'nav' pool.

Bede and Kearns got the fighter version. Ålvik got the Tse-Tse. Luwzinsky also chose the Tse-Tse.

Eventually all pilots were allocated their navigators. Some got on immediately. Others had to work at it. A few didn't work out at all, and had to be changed.

Strictly speaking, Smythe was not due to fly the mission; but he insisted on being included in the training. After all, he reasoned, he needed to continuously check the feasibility of his plan. He was given a pilot called Brace. Brace was twenty-one years old.

No one was permitted to talk about any aspect of the training to anyone outside the squadron crews. The Mosquitoes flew throughout the day and into the early evenings. Then came night flying. No one crashed, but two crews washed out. One crew had no co-ordination whatsoever, and the pilot of the other simply could not get to grips with the Mosquito.

Both Kearns and Bede had drawn navigators they could work with. Bede had once again become Kearns's wingman.

Ålvik took to the Mosquito easily. He was very pleased with the Tse-Tse, and as the only person who was truly familiar with the place they would eventually be attacking, looked forward to using that formidable gun against enemy ships in his homeland.

October 1943
The weeding out of the crews was complete. After nearly a month of intense flying, exactly eighteen crews – including Smythe and Brace – were deemed fit to continue into full operational training.

When all eighteen aircraft had landed one afternoon after a cross-country sortie, Bede said to Kearns, 'I wonder how my Mossie would handle a 190.'

'You're not hungry for a fight, are you?'

'Tell you what.'

'What?'

'I'm hungry for a fight.'

'A Mossie's not a Spit, James.'

'My Mossie's got two bloody great Merlin 25 engines pumping out 1635hp each. She's got *eight* guns, four of which are cannon. She's light on the controls, and without external stores I can fling her around. You saw how that Mossie that visited us about a hundred years ago was leaping around. Wouldn't it be a good way to find out how she performs in a real fight?'

'What are you suggesting?'

'I know the Mossie's supposed to be a long-range intruder, a long-range day fighter, a long-range night fighter, and whatever else can be rigged up for it in someone's fevered mind. I know other crews have had great successes with it in these roles . . .'

'What are you *really* getting at, James?'

'You and I. A quick prowl.'

'You mean go looking for trouble.'

'Well . . .'

'I'm the deputy CO. I'm supposed to be a responsible person.'

'You are. If this target is as tough as we all believe it to be, I have a feeling we're all going to need to know how close to the edge we can take the Mossie. Some of the things we may have to do won't be in the handling notes. Shouldn't a responsible deputy CO be trying to find out?'

'Nice argument, Bede!' Kearns said drily. 'Why do I have the feeling I'm being dragged into one of your wilder . . . Does your nav know about your suicidal inclinations?'

'Bede's navigator was a former Blenheim nav, a Dutchman named Laurens Koos, from Hilversum.

'He does,' Bede said, 'and is game.'

'He probably will be game. Game that's been shot.'

'Oh come on, Jo-Jo. We might learn something valuable that we can use on the mission itself.'

'All right,' Kearns said. 'I'll talk to the CO, and Wing Commander Smythe. If they say no . . .'

'Thanks, Jo-Jo!' Bede said and hurried away, as if afraid Kearns might change his mind.

Kearns shook his head slowly. 'Mad.'

But when he raised the suggestion with Smythe, he was surprised by the response.

'Good idea,' Smythe said. 'You'll be top cover for the raid on the day. You may well have to tangle with 190s. Go high. See what she'll do. All the aircraft have the Merlin 25. It would be a good way to check performance under combat conditions.'

Kearns looked at Luwzinsky.

'I think you should,' the CO said. 'Better find out now if we've got an Achilles' heel, than over the target.'

'Since we're all crazy,' Kearns said, 'I'll take Bede on the prowl tomorrow.'

Kearns's navigator was a Frenchman called Rameau, who, unlike his eighteenth-century namesake, was totally unmusical; but he shared a great passion with Ålvik. He, too, had been a member of the resistance in his own country, before escaping to England.

Prior to joining the resistance he had been a pilot flying the Dewoitine 250, the best single-seater fighter France had produced. In the frantic time of the invasion of his country, he had been up there, taking his own toll of the invaders' aircraft. Before the surrender the fast little fighter, in the hands of the French pilots, had destroyed nearly 150 of the enemy for the loss of just over eighty. But forty-four pilots had lost their lives.

Just before the collapse, Rameau had been shot down. He had got out of the stricken aircraft cleanly, but had landed in trees, dislocating an arm. Found by the members of the growing resistance movement, he had remained to fight. Though the arm functioned properly, he sometimes experienced sharp twinges. He had been turned down for further flying duties as a pilot; but his determination to continue flying had put him in the navigator's seat. He was already an experienced Mosquito nav. Though the official name for the second crewman in a Mosquito was 'observer', Rameau, like all the other unit navs who had made the grade, hated the term.

When Kearns had told Rameau what was planned for the next day, the Frenchman had simply said, 'You are going over *France*? Fantastique!'

They were cruising at 30,000 feet.

The Focke-Wulfs made it to that height with 7000 feet to spare, but that did not worry them. All the unit's aircraft could reach 40,000. It would take any 190s some time to get to that altitude; enough time to prepare for the engagement.

Kearns glanced out of the cockpit at Bede's aircraft. Like the days when they went hunting over the Channel, Bede was once more keeping perfect station. The Mosquito, with its engines underslung in long nacelles beneath that great wing, and its slim body, looked like an elegant moth on the whiteness.

Its wingspan of fifty-four feet two inches was greater by nearly twenty feet than the Spitfire's general average of thirty-six feet ten inches, and at forty and a half feet, its length exceeded the Spitfire's by over ten feet six inches. Despite this increase in overall size and weight, Bede was still able to keep as tight a formation as ever. He was so close that Kearns could see him clearly.

Bede looked across and gave a thumbs up. Kearns responded.

'He likes a good fight, your friend,' Rameau said from the nav's seat on the right.

'He likes something. Keep your eyes peeled, Jacques, if things get hot. I want you to make sure we don't lose sight of any Huns we find.'

'I will look. Do not worry. I hope we get a few Boche today.'

'I'll be happy with one.'

They seemed to be suspended over a cloud bank that stretched in all directions. Over to their right, a high white tower billowed in static majesty, probing the lofty blue of the sky above them.

With the cloud bank a good 10,000 feet below them, they flew deeper into French airspace, but no enemy aircraft put in an appearance.

They can't pick us up on their radar, Kearns thought. They don't know we're here.

He was not certain whether this was so, but wondered whether the bonded wood construction could be the reason. But soon after, two dots appeared above the whiteness, growing rapidly.

'Looks as if we've got trade, Jacques,' he said to his companion. 'Time to get your eyes working.'

'They are ready.'

Kearns glanced across at Bede, who made a forward motion with a hand. Bede had seen them too.

Without drop tanks, the aircraft were sleek and light. Time to find out what they could do.

He reached to his left for the supercharger gear-change switch at the rear of the throttle quadrant, and switched the two-stage superchargers from MOD to AUTO. They went immediately into high gear. His left hand then moved to the top of the quadrant for the throttle levers and smoothly eased them forwards until the engines were at 2650rpm and a boost reading of 7lb per square inch. This gave him maximum continuous operation. At a boost of 18lb and 3000rpm, he would be using full combat power, but with a time limit of just five minutes.

A glance to his right showed that Bede's aircraft had also begun to accelerate. It was like their old Channel patrol days, as if Bede had never been away. The instinctive way they worked together was back.

The small dots had grown and were still climbing. Kearns reached beneath the under-carriage lever on the main instrument panel and pressed the gun master switch.

'Camera.'

Rameau reached to his right for the gun camera switch, turned that on, and set the change-over button to CAMERA.

'You have camera,' he confirmed.

'Roger,' Kearns acknowledged.

Pressing either the control column thumb trigger for the machine-guns, or the finger trigger for the cannon would operate the camera. He was ready.

The dots had become Fw-190s and, still in the climb, they began to split right and left. But Kearns and Bede were waiting for that move.

Bede barrel-rolled sharply right, losing altitude abruptly and forcing the incoming 190 to counter. Having lost momentum in the climb, it was too slow to react and Bede was already back at the top of the barrel, with the 190 nicely pinned against the backdrop of the cloud bank.

Bede brought the nose down, tracking the 190 as it tried to roll away into the cloud. But the Mosquito was dropping rapidly now, closing the range swiftly. The 190 had nearly made it into the cloud when Bede pressed the thumb trigger, then squeezed the trigger for the cannon.

The alternate chatter and thump made an

unholy chorus as the eight guns hurled their lethal cargo at the 190. The combined discharge tore into the enemy aircraft just as it plunged into cloud.

At first, Bede thought he had missed. Then a sudden billow of black erupted out of the cloud bank. No flash of flame showed, but the black plume continued to hang above the undulating sea of white.

'We got him,' Koos said. There was awe in his voice. 'I have never seen anything like this. You were so quick.' He was looking at Bede, as if seeing him anew.

'This was not one of my really quick days,' Bede said lightly. He patted the instrument panel as they turned away from the dark banner of their victim. 'She's no Spitfire, but she's no slouch either. And she bites! I think I like her. Now where has Jo-Jo got to?'

Kearns was fully occupied with following the second 190 in a spiral dive.

The Mosquito tended to become very tail-heavy when diving at speed; but the spiral kept the speed within limits and continuous forward trimming kept the controls light as they plunged. Then abruptly, the Focke-Wulf stopped spiralling and went into a straight dive.

'He wants to get away!' Rameau exclaimed.

'Or he wants to draw us into a trap where his friends might be waiting. Look out for Bede.'

Rameau checked over his right shoulder. 'Behind us, coming down also.'

'Blue Two,' Kearns called. 'Stay up and watch for fish.'

'Roger,' Bede responded. His Mosquito pulled out of the dive.

The Focke-Wulf plunged into the cloud bank. Kearns followed.

'All right, Jacques. See if you can find him on the radar. Just a brief search.'

'I have him,' Rameau said after a short while. 'He is still ahead.'

'What's he playing at?'

'Ah!'

'What? What?'

'I have lost him.' Rameau sounded mortified.

'Don't worry about it. He's not going anywhere.'

'Blue One!'

'Blue One,' Kearns said, responding to Bede's call.

'Fish just popped. Ten o'clock.'

'Blue One,' Kearns acknowledged as he hauled the Mosquito back up through the cloud.

They cleared the top just in time to see the 190 wheel round to come towards them. In the distance was Bede's Mosquito. The Focke-Wulf pilot had clearly been surprised to find the other Mosquito sitting up top, and was wheeling away only to find Kearns charging towards him.

Tracers began to stream from the 190 as it rushed for a head-on pass.

Kearns went into a high barrel roll and watched through the top of the cockpit as the smaller fighter charged through the invisible tube he'd drawn in the sky. He eased left rudder to slice downwards. Heavy ruddering was not a smart thing to do in a Mosquito.

His manoeuvre had cut into the 190's reversal as it came back at him. This had positioned him just above the Focke-Wulf's spine as he came round. He tracked into it, tightening the turn to keep the 190's cockpit in sight. He knew he had to shoot quickly before the other aircraft reversed once more to slide away, and try to get on to his tail.

Beside him, Rameau waited tensely. The Merlins sang sweetly, never missing a beat as Kearns continued to haul into the turn.

The firing, when it came, startled Rameau who had been lulled by the siren music of the Merlins. Ahead of them, the machine-guns chattered and beneath their feet the four 20mm cannon thundered. Eight streams of tracer took the 190 along its spine, slamming into it like a brick wall hurled by a giant. The pulverizing blow opened up the 190 like a fish being filleted with a blunt knife. The teardrop canopy shattered, then the engine began to belch streamers of smoke as the rounds slammed past the cockpit and into the cowling. The enemy aircraft seemed to stop in mid-air. Then suddenly, nose and tail sections parted company, the two halves dropping towards each other as if the aircraft had been punched in the belly. Then they tumbled crazily towards the cloud bank, the tail faster than the forward section, which still had its wings attached. The nose fell steeply now, marking the sky with a streaming, expanding wake of black plumes as it disappeared into the cloud.

There was no flame, and no one got out.

'I think you killed the pilot,' Rameau said quietly.

'You don't sound happy,' Kearns said as he pulled into level flight and throttled back.

Rameau was searching the sky for more enemy aircraft.

'For one small moment,' he said, 'I did not think of him as a German who had invaded my country, but as an airman dying in that burst of fire. Do I make sense to you?'

'I understand,' Kearns told him soberly.

'But also, another part of me feels good. We have won the combat, and I am glad that he is dead.'

Kearns looked across and saw Bede's Mosquito slide into place.

'I know how you feel,' he said.

Whitehall, two days later
The men in the untidy office were studying their latest information on the ship. It was on the move. They contacted Photo Recce Command, and requested reconnaissance flights to find the *Graf von Hiller*.

They didn't.

A week after that the entire squadron flew to the Moray coast in Scotland, where they were to be based for the duration of the work up to the mission. They shared their base with other units, but were to remain completely autonomous. The embargo on discussing the mission with anyone outside the squadron was strictly maintained.

Impressed by the exploits of Kearns and Bede against the 190s, Smythe and Luwzinsky

detailed them to instruct all the other crews –
without exception – in the best way to employ
fighter tactics that maximized the strong points
of the Mosquito, the most prominent of which
was its tremendous fire-power.

'Never forget,' Kearns would say to them,
'you've got a killing machine at your fingertips.
Use it!'

Bede used the same exhortation, almost word
for word.

Training for the attack on the *von Hiller* was
carried out among the lochs, with the narrowest
that could be found being used to simulate the
Sognefjord, though they were not told this.

The purpose was to give the crews experience
in manoeuvring in confined spaces, with the
high ground standing in for anti-aircraft fire.
Hitting a rock wall was just as terminal as being
'bracketed' by a lethal burst of flak. Luwzinsky
and Kearns wanted them to manoeuvre instinctively, weaving past the dangers without pause,
flying at the edge of their skill. To hesitate
was to die.

All eighteen crews flew the same schedule, so
that each would be able to cope with changing
conditions during the attack. They flew low
over the water, almost skimming the surface

with the tips of the propellers. They shot their way up steep mountainsides, and plunged down again. They threaded their way through passes, wingtips pointing straight down. They carried out air-to-air manoeuvring against each other. Frequently, Bede or Kearns would spring an unexpected attack, then assess their chances of escape.

The non-stop training continued into November, when the winter came, and on into December.

Two days before Christmas a halt was called; but no one was allowed to go off the station. After Christmas training continued and on New Year's Eve Smythe summoned Ålvik.

The Norwegian entered the wing commander's office to find Luwzinsky and Kearns there as well.

Smythe indicated an empty chair and said, 'Please take a seat, Per.' And when Ålvik had done so, he continued, 'We're all very impressed with the way you've handled your flying. It's also been noted that you have a special affinity for low flying, but we would appreciate it if you and that Kiwi navigator of yours, McLeish, would refrain from bringing back other people's washing on your wings.'

'A strong wind had blown it aloft, sir,'

Ålvik said, straight-faced. 'We . . . flew into it.'

'Flew into it. I see. Well, let's see how you handle this. How would you like to lead the Tse-Tse flight?'

Ålvik stared, scarcely daring to believe it. 'I would very much like to, sir,' he replied eagerly, then glanced at Luwzinsky. 'But isn't Wing Commander Luwzinsky . . . ?'

'I thought that as we're going into your backyard,' Luwzinsky said, 'you should have the lead.' He smiled briefly. 'Besides, you do know your way around.'

'Thank you very much, sir!' Ålvik said gratefully. 'I shall not let you down.'

'I know you won't. We're handing you one of the most dangerous parts of the mission. Your job will be to attack the anti-aircraft defences repeatedly, while the ship is bombed and rocketed. This means going after the flak guns both along the fiord *and* on the ship itself.'

'I will do it,' Ålvik said firmly.

'Good man,' Smythe told him.

'I will fly as your number two,' Luwzinsky said.

Ålvik was genuinely touched by this show of confidence in him. 'Again, I can only thank you for giving me the opportunity to strike back at the people who invaded my country and destroyed my family. Thank you,' he finished in a voice that had gone very soft.

Smythe got up from his chair and went over and patted Ålvik on the shoulder. 'We're with you. Now, Wing Commander Luwzinsky has an idea about the attack. You know the topography of the area. We'd like to know what you think. Let's go to the map room.'

They all went into a smaller, adjoining room. A cold wind was coming off the Arctic and hurtling down the Moray Firth. It howled sobbingly outside.

'Let's hope we don't have this wind when the day comes,' Kearns said with feeling.

No one said anything to that, but their faces mirrored their thoughts. They all shared the same hope. Things would be ferocious enough in the fiord.

A large-scale map of the Sognefjord area was spread out on a large table. They went over to it, the three senior officers standing back to allow Ålvik to study the map closely. All along the sides of the fiord, red markers had been placed where anti-aircraft positions were expected to be. Various oval shapes, to signify naval units, were placed in the fiord itself. A big oval was at its head. This was the *Graf von Hiller*.

Ålvik scrutinized the map silently for nearly three minutes. At last he straightened and turned to face them.

'The big ship . . . ?'

'Is the *Graf von Hiller*,' Smythe replied. 'It is more powerful than the *Bismarck*, even though it's a relatively small vessel. It's specific job is to decimate the Allied invasion fleet. That's our target. I do not have to tell you what it would mean to the war effort if we fail.'

'The invader would stay longer in my homeland.'

'Among all the others . . . yes.'

Ålvik nodded slowly, understanding full well that the war could be prolonged if the *von Hiller* did succeed in wreaking havoc on the fleet.

'The flak and other AA,' he said, 'are where I would expect them to be. When I was with the resistance, the SS lieutenant colonel in command was replaced by a Wehrmacht officer who was not brutal, but very clever. A good tactician. He set up hunter-killer teams that wiped out most of the groups in the area, including mine. When I left, only four of us of my old group were still alive. I believe this same man is now in command of the defences around the fiord. Before I joined this squadron, I used to get news from home. I had to leave someone. But of course, because of our mission . . .'

'I'll have one of our people check with the Norwegian people in London,' Smythe said. 'See if there's anything for you.'

'Thank you, sir.'

'I think I may know something of the German commander you mentioned,' Smythe went on. 'What you've said confirms a little of what we do know.' He leaned over the map. 'Harry Luwzinsky believes we should make a multi-point attack, instead of running the gauntlet of the fiord. Where would you place the best points of entry?'

Ålvik again studied the map, then looked at Luwzinsky. 'How would the aircraft attack, sir?'

'In pairs, or even singly, all at different intervals, but not more than a second or two apart, and from different directions and heights. The idea is to confuse the defences. Give them so many targets, they may even shoot at each other, especially if we're low down. If there are many ships in the fiord, that may well happen as they try to track us. All attacks will, of course, be carried out at speed.'

'In that case,' Ålvik said, 'we may have many options. There will be places where the flak will be minimal. We can use the high ground to hide until the last moment. There are two places at the head of the fiord where the ship could take refuge. All the way to Årdalstangen . . . here. Or at Laerdal . . . here. They would not put it close to Laerdal but here at the junction of the Laerdalsfjord and the Årdalsfjord. They could also put it nearer the sea in that bend here, at Balestrand – but I think not. I would say one of the first two.

'If they do this, we can come at them from many quarters. As a resistance fighter I covered this whole area, and much more. There were not many soldiers, or guns. Of course, this new commander could have changed it; but I still think he will concentrate on the fiord. He will expect the attack to come from the sea, not from occupied territory. This will give us a big element of surprise. We will not be able to escape everything, but it will not be as hot as coming all the way up Sognefjord.'

Smythe nodded as Ålvik finished speaking. 'Once we've woken them up, of course, all hell will break loose. All right, Per. Draw up a plan of attack, based on your knowledge of the area.'

'I can stay in here to do this?'

'Certainly.'

'I will use this map.'

'Feel free to do so.'

Ålvik nodded. 'I will start right away.'

'Very well. Anything you need, just shout. We'll leave you to it.'

'Yes, sir.'

As they were leaving, Ålvik called, 'Squadron Leader Kearns . . .'

Kearns paused. 'I'll be along,' he said to the wing commanders.

They nodded and went out.

Kearns waited for the Norwegian to speak.

'Some time ago,' Ålvik began, 'you said if I had some private matters to discuss . . .'

'The offer still stands.'

'You heard me say to the wing commander that I left someone behind.'

Kearns nodded.

'She is someone very special,' Ålvik went on. 'She was in my resistance group. When I had to leave because the Germans were getting close, I asked her to come with me. She refused. She knew I was coming over to fly and said I had to do it, but that she should stay to carry on the fight the best way she knew how. We had all decided that the remaining four should go our separate ways, to avoid capture. The Germans were looking for a team, not individuals. They didn't know what the others looked like; but they knew me, because of what happened to my family. They tortured and raped my sister, and my fiancée . . .'

'Sweet Jesus . . .'

'Not the men of the new commander, but the SS. I feel guilty about leaving Inge. I keep thinking that if she falls into their hands, the same thing will happen to her. The SS are still there, you see, if the Wehrmacht officer is now in command of the fiord defences. Inge is not afraid of danger. She has had close shaves, but without me there . . .'

'Steady on, mate. The best thing you can do for her is to help us get that ship. Think of her when you go in to attack; but not of what you think *might* be happening to her. You've got the lead of your flight, and we're depending on you to give us the best points of entry. What would Inge want you to do?'

'Attack.'

'Precisely.'

'When they took my fiancée, I built a wall around myself. I had no feelings. Then Inge came.'

'And now you feel vulnerable.'

'Yes.'

'Tell you something, Per. There's nothing wrong with that.'

'*You* do not look vulnerable.'

'Don't you believe it, mate. One day, when this is all over, I'll tell you *my* story.' Kearns glanced at his watch. 'Oh.' He held out a hand. 'And Happy New Year.'

They shook hands.

9

Late April 1944

Smythe stood on a podium, before a huge photograph of a ship underway. Around the edges of the photo were white puffs that looked like scattered clouds. He looked at the assembled crews before him.

'Gentlemen,' he said, using a long pointer to tap at the image of the ship, 'the *Graf von Hiller*. Your target.'

There was a collective sharp intake of breath.

'As well you might,' he continued. 'Despite the quality of the photograph, which had to be taken in a hurry, those white things you see are not clouds, but a veritable carpet of flak. No doubt you'll be asking yourselves whether it's thick enough to walk on.'

There were a few nervous chuckles, but

they soon died. Most people were too stunned
to react.

'You have been very patient,' Smythe continued, 'and you have worked very hard over
the past months to maintain your very high
standards of skill. I'm proud of you all. You will
now begin to understand why you were pushed
so hard during the work-up to operational
capability. That ship is the most formidable
vessel afloat today, barring an aircraft carrier.
But an aircraft carrier's real teeth are her
aeroplanes. The *von Hiller*'s teeth are with
her all the time.

'We now know to a fairly certain extent that
the Hun intends to turn her loose on Allied
shipping before and during the invasion of
Europe, whenever that is due to begin. She
intends to raid from Norway to Spain, and
back. Her armament is such that she can
stand off and pulverize our ships without ever
coming close enough to be fired upon with any
effect. Our task is to stop her before she is fully
operational.

'We know she has now been deployed to
Norway, and is based in the Sognefjord. The
head of that fiord is *127 miles* inland. From
the sea to the target area, we can expect solid
anti-aircraft defences, on land as well as on the

surface, in addition to the *von Hiller*'s own defences. We can also expect fighters.'

There were a few groans.

'Yes, yes. I know,' Smythe said easily. 'We can't have Christmas every day.'

That brought a few louder chuckles.

'However, all is not as desperate as it might seem at first glance. The *von Hiller* is not yet a fully functioning ship. She has not yet had the time to turn her crew into a well-oiled machine . . .'

'Not like us!' someone shouted.

The laughter came more easily now.

'My thoughts precisely,' Smythe said, catching the mood smoothly. 'Further, there will be several diversionary raids mounted all over occupied Europe to keep the Hun guessing, including Germany itself, which will receive the brunt of these attacks.'

There were cheers.

'But best of all,' Smythe continued, 'we have with us Flight Lieutenant Per Ålvik, who is not only Norwegian, but knows the area like the back of his hand, so to speak. He has devised ways to let us in via the back door.'

'*Good old Per!*' they shouted.

Ålvik grinned. He had received news that Inge was still free, and in good health.

'The one thing we have not done,' the wing commander carried on, 'is to activate any resistance people in the area, or to send in saboteurs. It was imperative that no attention whatsoever be drawn to the ship. We intend to catch them napping.'

'Put the bastards to sleep for good!' came another shout.

'That will be up to us. Your flight commanders will give you the route to target. Take-off is at 0400 hours. Good luck, gentlemen. And now, the met officer.'

'*Get off!*' they yelled at the hapless meteorological officer when he had climbed the podium.

'They're in good spirits,' Smythe said to Luwzinsky and Kearns outside the briefing room.

The met officer was being mercilessly barracked.

'How many of them will be back after this?' Luwzinsky wondered. 'Or us, for that matter. Which reminds me,' he continued to Smythe. 'You said "us" during your speech. You were supposed to fly during training, but not go on ops.'

'You're not thinking of grounding me,

are you, Harry? You need every aircraft and crew.'

'You planned this from the beginning,' Luwzinsky said. 'You knew we would get to this point.'

'If I'm going to send people into a cauldron, I can hardly stay behind.'

'That's what planners *are* supposed to do.'

'Too late, Harry. I pre-empted you. I got my permission from the Air Ministry long ago.'

'You sneaky devil.'

'That's what planners are. Sneaky.'

Sognefjord, Norway

General Delsingen could see the ship clearly from his headquarters. The steep sides of the ancient flooded valley that was the fiord made it a perfect haven. He had sited anti-aircraft guns all along the route. If the enemy attacked, there would be a heavy price to pay.

But the scene was so peaceful that it was almost hard to imagine that the graceful ship out there was, in reality, little more than a representation of the zenith of naval killing machines.

Never one to take anything for granted, Delsingen had also sited listening posts at strategic points. However, he did make a mistake. He would eventually realize this far too late for him to have any hope of rectifying it.

A familiar knock on his door was followed by Geissler's entry.

'Any news of the Allied landings in France?' Delsingen asked of his subordinate, certain there would be.

Geissler shook his head. 'None, sir. There are no full-scale landings. It's almost quiet down there, by all accounts.'

'Make no mistake, Colonel,' Delsingen said. 'There will be a landing.'

'I have other news.'

'Go on.'

'There has been an escalation of the bombing at home.'

Delsingen nodded. 'The whirlwind, Geissler. It's getting closer. Look at that ship out there. It's a beautiful monster, isn't it? But it won't make much of a difference. Oh, it could probably damage the Allied fleet very badly, and the war might continue for another year or two. But what do you think our cost will be?'

'I try not to think of it, General.'

'You're a wise man, Ernst. Such things *are* better left unthought. I want you to make one of your trips to Bergen. I don't trust Mindenhof to behave himself if we don't keep him on his toes. Fröhmann's E-boat is here. Tell him he's got my authority to take you. Or would you prefer to fly?'

'I think I'll take the boat trip. Seems a nice fresh day for it. I'll enjoy the fast journey on the fiords. Fröhmann always likes to show me what it can do. We'll be there by morning.'

'All right. Do you want to take a couple of men with you? Just in case Mindenhof gives you a problem?'

'In a strange way, I don't think he'd dare. He's got what he wants. He feels he can now afford to humour you.'

'I'll give you some of your own advice, Colonel. Be careful.'

'Yes, sir.'

The E-boat powered past the *Graf von Hiller*.

'Every time I see that ship I still can't believe it,' Geissler said as they seemed to be going on and on past the battleship. It towered above their vessel, making it seem like a toy. 'It's so huge! And all those guns!'

'She's quite something,' Fröhmann agreed, 'but give me this little beauty any day. I'd hate to be aboard the *von Hiller* when she turns turtle. Imagine trying to get out from below decks. All that armour. All that weight. No thanks. I like my little sports runabout. She's fast, and she's lethal. Good enough for me.'

'But the *Graf von Hiller* is not going to turn turtle.'

'You believe she is unsinkable? Remember the *Titanic*. That was "unsinkable" too. There's no such thing.'

They were approaching the boom of the first anti-submarine barrier.

'Zuchner!' Fröhmann called to the man at the wheel.

'*Wohl, Herr Kapitän!*'

'*Beide Maschinen langsam!*'

'*Beide Maschinen langsam, Herr Kapitän!*'

The E-boat dropped its raised prow as they slowed for the passage through the boom which was being opened to let them through. They repeated the procedure through two more, then they were free of obstacles.

Fröhmann ordered the helmsman to take it back to full speed and the E-boat roared down the fiord.

They passed two destroyers, the outer screen of the battleship's defence.

As the E-boat churned throatily along, its red, white and black swastika ensign fluttering stiffly at its mast, Fröhmann said, 'This is what

I like most about this war. Sailing at speed on the fiords. I wish I could do this just for enjoyment.'

'Why don't you come back when the war is over?'

'And when might that be?'

'It must end sometime.'

'And who will give me an E-boat in which to enjoy myself?'

Geissler smiled. 'You've got me there.'

'So we enjoy it now.'

'All right, Fröhmann. You win.'

The naval officer grinned.

They would arrive in Bergen about an hour after the Mosquitoes had taken off on their mission to sink the *Graf von Hiller*.

Moray Coast, Scotland. 0400 hours

Kearns and Rameau sat in their Mosquito as the engines warmed up. Already, the first flight of six – the fighter-bombers – were on their take-off run, doing so one after the other in the dim twilight of the coming dawn.

'No turning back now, Jacques,' Kearns said.

'No. We will have some fun, eh?'

'We'll do our very best.'

The eighteen aircraft were arranged as Yellow Flight, the fighter-bombers; Red Flight,

the Tse-Tses; and Blue Flight, the fighters for
escort. Smythe, though a navigator, had the
lead of Yellow. Luwzinsky, though still in
overall command of the squadron, had already
passed the lead of Red Flight to Ålvik. Blue
Flight was commanded by Kearns, with Bede
as his number two.

He watched as the first six took off without
mishap. Then it was the turn of Red Flight.

Red One, Ålvik, began his take-off run,
followed by Luwzinsky. Then it all began to
go wrong.

'*Burst tyre! Burst tyre!*' Kearns heard in his
headphones. '*Blue One! You have command!
Blue One! You have command!*'

Kearns watched in horror as Red Two, piloted
by Luwzinsky, began to swing off the runway. It
was going much too fast to stop safely. He could
imagine the squadron commander fighting for
his life and his navigator's, trying desperately
to correct the swing. But the fuel-laden aircraft
hit something on the ground and pivoted about
a wingtip. A sheet of flame twice as long as the
Mosquito suddenly shot out. It curled on itself
to lick at the gyrating aeroplane. There was
a sudden vivid explosion and the Mosquito
seemed to vanish in the flames. There was no
chance for the crew.

'Oh my God!' Kearns said softly.

Then he roused himself. He was in command now. Nothing he could do about what had just happened. Time to think about it later. The mission had to be continued.

'All aircraft. This is Blue One! You heard the man. Carry on with your take-off.' He wondered how Per Ålvik, who had been so close to the tragedy, now felt as he lifted his aircraft into the air.

There were now only five Tse-Tse Mosquitoes to take on the guns.

'Let's hope the back door works,' Kearns said to Rameau. 'Per is one down.'

'We must not think about it.'

'No.'

Red Flight were airborne.

'Our turn, Jacques.'

Bergen, 0600 hours

The E-boat cruised slowly into the inner harbour. Geissler saw the girl sitting on the sea wall and wondered what she was doing there so early in the morning. Then he saw a squad of SS men marching purposefully towards her.

'Fröhmann!' he called sharply.

Startled by the urgency in his voice, the naval officer turned quickly. 'What?'

'Get me ashore. Fast!'

'What is happening?'

'I'm not sure, but I intend to stop it.'

Geissler himself had no idea why he was behaving in such a manner. He simply had a feeling that the girl was about to get into trouble. For some reason, he didn't want that to happen.

'Come on! Hurry!'

'All right, all right! Why the sudden panic anyway?' Then Fröhmann saw where Geissler was looking. 'Aha! Pretty! Friend of yours?'

'No.'

'But . . .'

'Please! Before those SS men get to her.'

The girl seemed quite unaware that the four men were bearing down on her.

'Be careful, Colonel. These SS are a law unto themselves.'

'I'll be all right.'

The E-boat was brought close to the pier. Geissler leapt out almost before it was close enough.

'*You!*'

The girl turned, as if seeing the SS men for the first time. She did nothing else.

'*Stand up, bitch!*' the squad leader snarled in bad Norwegian. He was an *Untersturmführer*

– a second lieutenant – young, full of himself and out to impress his men. '*A German officer is talking to you!*'

She remained seated, and said quietly, 'And a Norwegian is sitting on her harbour wall.'

'*Do you want to be kicked into the water?*' he screamed at her.

'No,' she said, still calm.

The men in the squad were smiling surreptitiously. It was difficult to tell whether they were secretly laughing at her or the lieutenant. They began to eye her with more than passing interest, assessing possibilities.

'Then stand up, or you will be dragged up! What are you doing here? This is a restricted area!'

She stood up, slowly. 'Stop shouting. I'm not deaf.'

'No insolence!' He raised a hand to strike her.

'*Lieutenant!*'

He jerked in the act of striking, frozen by this unexpected interruption.

Geissler hurried up to them. 'What do you think you're doing?'

'This woman was insolent, *Herr Oberstleutnant.* I was about to teach her some manners. She is also in a restricted area.'

'You were correct in apprehending her. I shall take it from here.'

'With respect, *Herr Oberstleutnant*. I must insist . . .'

'*You what?*' Geissler roared so suddenly that all four SS men gave an involuntary jump. 'How dare you, Lieutenant! You will give me the respect properly due to my rank or you'll find yourself on the Eastern Front before your heels next touch the ground. *Is that clear?*'

The SS second lieutenant looked into Geissler's eyes, saw the coldness in them, noted the Iron Cross ribbon, and did a rapid rethink.

'I apologize to the Colonel!' he said stiffly.

His men smirked.

'Now move on!'

'Move!' the lieutenant barked at his men, his face suffused with anger and embarrassment.

'You must like living dangerously,' a voice said. 'Even though he is a little pipsqueak, he's still SS, and Mindenhof is still in charge.'

Geissler turned and saw Fröhmann. He had two armed sailors with him.

'Is that why they left?'

'No. They were doing that before we came on the scene.'

They all looked at the girl.

She was staring at Geissler. 'Why did you do that?'

'You speak German.'

'You lot have been here long enough. It's inevitable.'

'Are you crazy? What are you doing here at this time of the day?'

'I was taking a walk. I stopped. This is my country.'

'A very patriotic attitude that can get you killed.'

'So why did you stop them? You are German.'

Geissler looked at her thoughtfully. 'You're not afraid of me, are you?'

'No.'

'Or of the SS?'

'No.'

'You should be.'

'Why? Don't they die like everyone else?'

The sailors were staring at her disbelievingly, clearly thinking she was insane.

Fröhmann looked on amused. 'You can go back to the boat,' he told the sailors. 'Thank you.'

They gave the girl another bemused look, before returning to the E-boat.

'I don't know what you want here,' Geissler

said to her, 'but get away before a more senior
SS man comes.'

'You are afraid of the SS?'

'No! And stop these stupid questions. Come
on. Get away from here!'

She seemed surprised by his attitude. 'You
really don't want them to get me, do you?'

'Move!'

'All right. I'm going.' She stared almost
unnervingly at him. 'What happened to her?'
she asked softly.

'Wha . . . what? What are you talking
about?'

'You lost someone, once.'

Then she turned and walked away.

Geissler watched her go, feeling as if a ghost
had visited him.

'You seem pale, Geissler,' the E-boat captain
said. 'Are you all right?'

'Yes, yes. I'm fine.'

'What did she mean?'

'I have no idea.'

Inge Jarl watched the two German officers
walk away.

She'd seen all she'd needed to, and would
pass the information on down the line. She
had been in the area for two days. Her mission

had been to observe what was going on, and report. She had no idea why this information was needed at this time. She didn't like this work and preferred to be in the field, fighting. She missed Per and hoped he was still flying and safe. The incongruity of these two wishes did not trouble her.

Had the SS men searched her, they would have found a pistol. She knew she had nearly taken one chance too many. If it hadn't been for that Wehrmacht officer . . . Strange, she thought. He had really been frightened of letting the SS take her away. Had he really let a woman down before? Someone who had loved him?

She began to make her way out of the area, resolving never to take such a stupid risk again. She would ask not to be sent on any more such assignments.

Her body ached for Per.

'Strange,' Ålvik said.

'What is?' Kiwi McLeish asked.

'Oh, I just thought of someone.'

'Is she pretty?'

'Is it so obvious?'

'Oh yes.'

Ålvik looked out of the cockpit to check

the sky about him. All he could see were
Mosquitoes.

'They look good,' he said.

'Don't they just?' the New Zealander agreed.
'You must feel good going back to the old
country to bang a few Jerry heads together.'

'Yes, I do.'

'Bad luck about the CO.'

'Yes. Very bad luck. He was a good man.
Dennis, too. The good always go first.'

'So we're going to be around for a while,
eh?' McLeish said, laughing. The sound was
bizarre in his mask.

'Perhaps,' Ålvik said.

But he smiled.

Ålvik's plan had worked – so far. He had
also been right about where the ship would
be anchored.

They crossed the Norwegian coast on opposite sides of the fiord, routeing well away from
the target area. The bombers, carrying armour-
piercing, very high-explosive bombs, some with
delayed-action fuses, would be approaching the
target from Årdalstangen.

The Tse-Tses would come from two directions: Laerdal and across from Kaupanger. The
fighters would go high, initially, then apparently

disappear, only to join in the fun at very low level. If fighters appeared, they would engage. The primary task was the ship and to get the bombs on.

Smythe could not believe they were still unde-tected and thanked every deity that Ålvik knew the area so well.

'Two minutes to target,' he said to Brack.

'Yes, sir,' the young pilot acknowledged.

'Are you all right?'

Brack swallowed. 'I'm fine, sir.'

'We go in fast and very low, drop our bombs, then break right into the valley. Just as you were briefed. We'll be in there for mere seconds, and be gone before they know it.'

'Yes, sir.'

One of the soldiers manning one of the listening posts set up by Delsingen was staring at the formation of aircraft high above him. He spoke urgently into his radio.

'They look like small aircraft. Fighters. Not bombers. How should *I* know where they're going? Am I flying up there? They're heading east. East! Yes. Pass it on anyway. Let them do what they want with it. Then they can't say we didn't relay the information. Up here? It's cold, and I want a woman. What? Fat chance out here. The Norwegians hate us.'

He ended transmission and looked up again. The fighters had gone.

Kearns, having displayed his high formation for the benefit of ground watchers, ordered his aircraft to split into pairs. Each pair descended earthwards in different directions.

Desultory flak came up at them. None of the bursts was even close.

'It seems as if Per was right, after all,' he said to Rameau. 'Hardly any AA out here.'

'Let us be thankful for small blessings.'

'I am. Believe me. The first bombs should be going down about now.'

'Christ!' Smythe said. 'Just look at the size of that ship!'

They had erupted from cover and, incredibly, the surprise was so complete, not a single gun fired at them.

'*Bomb doors!*' Brack shouted.

Smythe was already reaching for the lever next to the undercarriage selector. '*Open!*'

Brack squeezed the release button. '*Bombs gone! Let's get out of here!*'

*   *   *

The crewmen on the deck of the *von Hiller* could not believe their eyes when the twin-engined aircraft came at them from *landward*. They assumed it was one of theirs. Only when they saw the objects dropping towards them and the great planform of the Mosquito as it banked away, showing its RAF roundels, did they realize what was happening.

They then started to run.

Brack had been far more successful than he would have dared hope. Not only had he got away scot-free with not a single shot being fired at him, but his first bomb went straight down a funnel, plunging deep into the bowels of the ship before exploding. The second followed the same path, adding to the carnage.

The first wounds had been inflicted.

Delsingen, from his vantage-point, had seen the aircraft suddenly appear, heading for the ship. Like the sailors, he had at first thought it to be a German aircraft, because it had come from such a totally unexpected quarter. Then he'd seen the bombs falling, heard the roar of the aeroplane, seen the RAF roundels, and had felt both a sense of despair and of the inevitable.

He had rushed to get his binoculars and

focused on the *Graf von Hiller*'s forward
funnel. A great sheet of flame had erupted
from it, shooting, it had seemed, hundreds of
feet into the air. A rumbling, muffled explosion
deep within had sent a visible tremor through
the ship, causing it to shift in the water as if
it had just fired a broadside.

Why weren't the ship's guns firing? he
wondered. And what of the flak batteries he
had sited all along the fiord? Were they asleep
out there?

Then the answer had come to him. There
was nothing for them to shoot at. The aircraft
that had launched the attack had gone.

In Delsingen's mind, time had stretched. What
seemed like several minutes was in fact fleeting
seconds. His mind had expanded the passing
moments into lengths of time where even the
smallest of events could be closely observed. It
was thus that he was able to watch – as if in slow
motion – the second aircraft go into the attack,
drop its bombs: one into the second funnel, the
other at its base. Again that aircraft pulled hard
to the right almost immediately, to escape any
possible anti-aircraft response.

Again no guns fired. Again a deep rumble
shook the ship, and again it shifted in the
water. Delsingen felt as if he alone could see

what was happening; as if everyone else had been frozen in time.

Then time seemed to regain its natural speed.

A pall of dense smoke was now pouring out of both funnels; but this was not because the *Graf von Hiller* was attempting to conceal herself. The precious battleship was beginning to bleed.

Someone knocked on the door and rushed into the office.

'*Herr General! The British are attacking the ship!*'

Delsingen turned to the young captain who had barged in. 'That's very observant of you, Schulenheim,' he said bitingly. 'Have you discovered why the batteries are not yet firing?'

'We've already contacted them, *Herr General*. They say there are no aircraft.'

'Then tell them there'll be more! This is only the beginning!'

'Yes . . . Yes, *Herr General*!'

'Well, don't just stand there, man! Get to it!'

'Yes, *Herr General*!'

'And find out what the observation posts are doing!'

'Yes, *Herr General*!'

As the captain hurried out, Delsingen reflected on the fact that he was finished, whatever the outcome. Even if all the aircraft were shot down and the *von Hiller* not too badly damaged, the attack would be seen as his fault. It had happened, and that would be enough for them to demand his head. In the current climate there was a high demand for scapegoats.

The High Command – particularly the SS High Command – would lay the blame squarely at his feet. Not even Honnenhausen would be able to save him. And Mindenhof would have a field day.

A new sound had broken into Delsingen's thoughts. A third aircraft, this time coming from the opposite direction, but not from up the fiord.

Delsingen once more brought the binoculars to his eyes. From where he stood, the twin-engined aeroplane seemed to have curved in from the right, popping out from hiding behind high ground. Clinically, his mind observed it as a beautiful sight, the way it banked swiftly and tightly, levelled off, released its bombs, then banked hard left to rush towards Årdalstangen and the safety of the mountains. He even marvelled at the courage of the pilot, coming in so low as to appear to touch the ship with his aircraft.

He saw the bombs fly towards the deck of the ship. One bounced, before lodging itself at the base of one of the forward turrets that housed two of the big fifteen-inch guns. The other flew right through the armoured glass of the bridge. They went off simultaneously. The bridge contained the explosion, but its sides bulged and then contracted in response to the percussive force of the blast. Delsingen didn't dare think of the fate of anyone who had been within that explosion. The *Graf von Hiller* seemed to shake itself, as if shrugging off this third blow.

The bomb by the armoured gun turret tilted it off line when it exploded, but that seemed to be all. The turret, though appearing to have escaped serious damage, would not be able to swivel until repaired.

A light Oerlikon had begun to fire, but there was nothing for it to shoot at.

There was another knock on the door, and Schulenheim rushed in once more.

Delsingen turned. '*Hauptmann* Schulenheim!' he barked.

Schulenheim skidded to a halt and stiffened to attention. '*Herr General!*'

'Stop running about like a schoolboy! You're an officer, man! You are supposed to behave calmly under attack and be an example to your subordinates. Now compose yourself and tell me why you have rushed into my office.'

'*Herr General*, only one observer post has so far made a report. The observer reported high-flying fighters.'

'Delsingen frowned. '*Fighters?*'

'Yes, *Herr General*. Going east.'

'Check with that man. Ask him to describe in detail what he saw, or what he *thought* he saw, then return immediately when you've got the answer.'

'Yes, *Herr General*.

'And find me Kahler.'

'Yes, *Herr General*.'

The captain went out again, and Delsingen returned to watching the ship.

'Fighters?' he murmured thoughtfully.

The aircraft that had dropped the bombs had been small for a bomber, twin-engined, highly manoeuvrable. Though he had never been on the receiving end of their attention before, he knew what Mosquitoes looked like. He knew of people who had been on the wrong end of an attack by them. They were deadly, and remarkably accurate. Those agile aeroplanes were also *fighters*, and an observer who knew little of the type would class them as such on seeing them for the first time.

But according to Schulenheim, they'd been high-flying . . .

A feint, of course. There would be more of them, and they could be anywhere. It was time to get Mölner to send his boys up and . . .

Delsingen stopped, mouth grim. Despite the fact that his *Sondergruppe* had been astoundingly successful, someone had made a decision to remove the air element. He could no longer order Mölner into the air. He would have to go through Luftwaffe channels, and that would lose precious time.

A swelling sound made him train the glasses back on the ship. More smoke was wreathing about it, but far from forming a protective curtain, the billows of smoke and steam from ruptured pipes were effectively marking it out.

A fourth aircraft had swung into the attack, coming from the same direction as the third. This time, people on the ship were more awake. The multi-barrelled cannon were now adding their voices to the proceedings. Tracers reached for the Mosquito, but seemed to be doing it no harm. The bombs curved in an accurate trajectory from the aircraft. Both went into the bridge, yet there was no immediate explosion.

Delayed action.

The thought came instinctively to Delsingen. He continued to watch, waiting for the inevitable explosion. It was not a long time in coming. The double explosion made the bridge well until it appeared that the entire superstructure would burst outwards. But that was not what happened. Incredibly, it *collapsed inwards*. It simply caved in, as if all supporting beams and girders had been melted by an intense heat. As it went, various radar and radio masts went with it, first swaying, then toppling on top of the imploding mass.

But the gunners had drawn blood. The Mosquito that had made the fourth attack was now towing a long, bright tail of flame that ravenously ate its way forwards along the fuselage. The aircraft tried to climb, as if to get away from the flames. The fire seemed to rush even faster towards the nose until the entire aeroplane had become a rising comet. Then it turned into a starburst that spread outwards like a giant firework, sending flaming pieces over a wide area. Some fell into the water, sending erupting gouts of steam shooting upwards.

Though cheered by the success of the gunners,

Delsingen again sensed a feeling of admiration for the airmen's bravery.

But the gunners were suddenly facing a new danger. As if from nowhere, another Mosquito was approaching the ship from water-level, it seemed. The sound of a massive cannon roared within the fiord. A huge tongue of flame belched from beneath the nose of the aircraft and something pulverizing slammed into the gunners' position. They disappeared in a bright inferno.

The Mosquito banked slightly, swinging round to a new target. Another belch, and another gun position vanished.

'My God!' Delsingen heard himself say. 'They're using a flying tank!'

Even as he spoke, yet another Mosquito could be seen diving steeply down the right side of the fiord. This one seemed to have come from straight over the top. It was another of the flying tanks, for it had now engaged a flak battery that had fired just once before being engulfed in a burst from the big cannon.

More batteries were now at last opening up, but more Mosquitoes seemed to have infested the fiord, roaming along its sides, wheeling into the guns and roaring at them with that huge cannon.

Delsingen went to grab at his phone, and called for the district Luftwaffe commander. He waited impatiently until the person who finally came on the line turned out to be the deputy, who sounded harassed. All fighter aircraft throughout southern Norway were up, he was told: sent to meet massive raids that spread southwards down to the Skagerrak and into Denmark.

Delsingen had to strain to listen to what was being said, as the cacophony of guns and aircraft engines swelled appreciably.

He stifled a sigh at the man's words. 'Send me whatever you can,' he said, 'when you can. Otherwise we'll lose the *Graf von Hiller*.'

'I'll do my best . . .'

'What about Mölner?'

'He's been up twice already, dealing with these raids. He's on his third scramble right now. It's very bad, General. I don't even know if we can . . .'

'Try and have him divert at least a flight of his fighters to this area. If we lose the ship many, many heads will roll.' Mine included, he didn't add.

'I'll do my best, General,' the other man repeated, but he didn't sound at all certain that he'd be able to.

'All right. Thank you.'

'General.'

They hung up together.

Delsingen stared at the phone, then went back to his vantage-point. The ship was already lost. Of that, he was quite certain.

The attack had been beautifully executed. The unexpected first approach had achieved complete surprise. The multi-point attack was sowing confusion, and the specialist anti-flak Mosquitoes were silencing the guns so as to allow the bombers to continue their work. Nor was there any doubt that the fighter Mosquitoes were around somewhere, waiting for any German fighters that might come to attack the raid.

But those fighters had been drawn away by diversionary raids of such magnitude that they could not have been ignored, effectively preventing the dispatch of fighters to protect the ship.

Someone had also known the area well enough to have correctly judged where the gaps in the anti-aircraft umbrella would be. The attacking Mosquitoes had thus been able to make their approach without warning. No one had spotted them except the sole observer who had seen the high-flying fighters. And that had been a deliberate disclosure, to further hide the true nature of the target. For no one would seriously expect fighters to attack a battleship.

The attackers had also picked a time well before the ship was ready for operations at sea. The crew still had to be fully trained; the gunners to be drilled and finely tuned, to go into action with confidence and skill. And worst of all, the *von Hiller*, trapped within her protective, triple anti-submarine screens, was like a big fish in a small barrel.

The Allies had discovered her existence and had correctly come to the conclusion that she would be used to cause havoc with the invasion fleet. They desired her destruction at any cost. Even if this raid did not succeed completely, there would be more, and still more.

The *Graf von Hiller* was going nowhere.

10

As these thoughts hurtled through his mind, Delsingen realized that even during the brief period that he'd been on the phone, things had hotted up considerably in the fiord.

There now seemed to be a continuing swarm of Mosquitoes, whirling and diving among the ships and guns. The flak in the fiord had grown into a ferocious barrage, staining the air with their shoals of bursts, and lacing the fiord with their tracers. Nothing, it seemed, could live through that.

But the bomber Mosquitoes were not straying far towards them. The guns were being constantly engaged by the aircraft with the tank guns and, every so often, a flak battery would be put out of action. Those further down the fiord were virtually useless, because the aircraft were not going there. They concentrated on the ship and its immediate environs, knocking out all the most threatening of guns while continuing the attack.

Flames were now springing up all over the pocket battleship. Rocket projectiles were pounding into her. It was like watching a great beast being harried by smaller, savage predators. She couldn't move and now could barely defend herself. Such guns as betrayed their presence by flashes in the ever-increasing billows of smoke, were instantly attacked and put out of action.

The tank-gun Mosquitoes were even attacking the destroyers as soon as the anti-aircraft guns on those ships opened up. But they flew so low that the gunners on the smaller ships could not bring their weapons to bear properly, or in time. Two E-boats that had come in the day before had also put up a fierce resistance with their multi-barrelled cannon. Both had been blown out of the water with a double attack by two of the tank-gun Mosquitoes. It was turning into a slaughter.

Then another Mosquito flamed into the fiord, diving straight in. At least, Delsingen thought grimly, the gunners were getting some small revenge.

He heard loud voices, then there was a loud knocking.

'*In!*'

Kahler, now a captain, entered looking exceedingly grim. He had his steel helmet under his arm.

'I got here as quickly as I could, General,' he began. 'I was attending to the guns, seeing that they put up enough high explosive to make life very dangerous for the Tommis. But, as you can see, the aircraft are keeping their attack concentrated around the ship. No one expected bombers that could manoeuvre like fighters.' The man who once had the bowel problem was radically changed. He had become every inch the confident warrior.

'You were right to get the guns started,' Delsingen said. 'As for the attack, it has been cleverly executed.'

Kahler gave a slight instinctive duck of the head as a swelling roar of engines passed right overhead. But the aircraft was not interested in the headquarters building, even though a burst of cannon fire from the nearby guns followed it.

'You should take shelter, General,' he suggested.

'Why? They're not interested in this place. Besides, I am not someone who goes into hiding.'

'They had precise information, sir,' Kahler went on. 'It's the only answer. They knew how to get into the area.'

Delsingen gave a rueful smile. 'Would you like to hear a crazy thought that has entered my head?'

Kahler was not sure how to respond to this, so he said nothing.

'Ålvik,' Delsingen told him.

'*Ålvik?*'

'You find that hard to believe?'

'But he must be dead by now.'

'No one ever found him. He could have gone to England. Many Norwegians go over, are trained in covert operations and return.'

'You're saying he is *here*, in Norway, General?'

'He may not be, but his extensive knowledge of this area may have been used.'

'He could not have known about the ship.'

'No. That would have come from somewhere else.'

Another aircraft, passing extremely low this time, made both of them duck. Again it did not attack the building.

'Colonel Geissler is lucky to be out of this,' Kahler said grimly, listening to the hellish noise that continued to echo round the fiord.

'That's a matter of opinion,' Delsingen said. 'There are enemies in Bergen too, and rather closer to home. All right, Captain. It's obvious you know what to do. Carry on.'

'Sir. General.'

Delsingen looked at him.

'It has been an honour serving in your command.'

'Thank you, Captain.'

'Sir.'

Kahler put on his helmet and saluted Delsingen with precise gravity.

Ålvik had ten shells remaining out of the twenty-five-round load of the big gun. The Tse-Tse could spit them at just over one a second. A two-second burst was usually enough for something like a soft-skinned boat, a gun emplacement or any target armoured like a tank.

But he was not diving on a tank. He had twice passed over a building from where streams of tracer from light guns had chased after him. He now decided to silence them, for they were on an access route to some of the other flak guns.

In the right-hand seat, McLeish was certain they were not going to make it this time. Ålvik may well know the topography of his country like the back of his hand, but the position of the anti-aircraft cannon by the squat building was too close to a steep mountainside. When they had twice flown over to attack the flak guns, they had nearly landed on the building, he'd thought. This time, they would probably hit it.

But he said nothing, not wanting to distract his pilot. He simply watched as the streams of tracer spurted towards them, wondering which of these would first punch a hole through the armoured windscreen, to be followed by the ones which would disintegrate his head.

These morbid thoughts in his mind, McLeish listened first to the machine-guns as they began to chatter, then to the single roar of the big gun as it belched, *at the building itself*. Then the Mosquito was pulling steeply away, before tipping over on a wing to come round again.

This time McLeish understood what Álvik was about. As they again approached the building he saw that a great part of it was no longer there; and only one gun, fully exposed, was still firing. A great cloud of rising dust came from where falling masonry had buried the other.

The big gun roared again, just once.

McLeish saw the explosion just as they flashed past. The anti-aircraft gun did not fire.

As the Mosquito changed course to go after

another flak battery, McLeish said, 'That was close.'

'Did you hold your breath?'

'Yeah,' the New Zealander replied frankly. 'I did.'

'So did I.'

Delsingen felt the dust in his mouth. Something incredibly heavy was on the small of his back. He tried to move, but all he could manage was a flutter of his fingers.

Had he been able to, he would have seen that most of his office had fallen on him. There was a gaping hole where one wall used to be, and the roof had disappeared. He would also have seen dust-covered people scrambling over piles of rubble to get to him.

Hearing voices faintly, he tried to turn his head. But it wouldn't move.

'I've found the General!' he heard very, very faintly, as if from a great distance.

'Get those things off him!' another voice ordered. It sounded like Kahler's. '*Hurry!*'

But Delsingen could hear nothing any more.

Jo-Jo Kearns was still keeping his flight of six Mosquitoes out of the fiord. Where were the fighters?

'It looks as if the diversionary raids have worked,' he said to Rameau. 'There's not a dicky-bird out there. Bede is going to get very impatient soon. He needs a charge of action every so often.'

Rameau peered out of the cockpit, to where a great column of smoke rose from below.

'The others are having fun,' he said. 'You have brought us your great luck, Jo-Jo. We have only lost two aeroplanes, and it seems we have got the ship.'

'Two are two too many. Counting the CO on take-off, that's three. I'd like to take the rest home. How long have we been out here?'

'Ten minutes from the start of the attack.'

'My God. It feels like ten years. I'd prefer to have them all out of there before any fighters turn up.'

Suddenly a vast, boiling explosion lit up the day. A great, bell-shaped, fiery cloud rose from the fiord, expanding as it went. From all directions, small shapes darted from the area. The Mosquitoes were making a hasty exit, so as not to be caught in the shock wave.

The fiery bell ruptured and burst open, sending a fierce, bright pillar of flame reaching for the heavens. Then a great cloud followed, boiling upwards, climbing for ever, it seemed.

Rameau gasped at the sight. *'The magazine! They have got the magazine! Ha-hah-hah-hah!'* he crowed with glee. 'The ship is gone! It's gone!' He was jumping about in his seat.

In the distance, the remaining Mosquitoes were rapidly heading to rendezvous with them.

'Herr Kapitän! Herr Kapitän!'

In Bergen, Geissler and Fröhmann were standing at the water's edge, in conversation. After the incident with the girl, Geissler had expected to see an enraged Mindenhof very soon after. But nothing had happened. Perhaps, he'd reasoned, Mindenhof had expected Geissler to come to him like some supplicant, now that he was in command of local security.

Fröhmann had turned to look at the agitated member of his crew who was running towards them.

'The ship, Herr Kapitän!' the man said in a rush. *'The* Graf von Hiller! *She is sunk!'*

'What?' both Geissler and Fröhmann shouted together.

'Yes, sir. There was an attack by British aeroplanes. E-62 was just entering the fiord when there was a great explosion. The ship just blew up, like the way the English lost the *Hood*. E-62 saw many small planes going away. They had hit the magazine. A great wave in the fiord, caused by the explosion, nearly capsized E-62. The *Graf* is gone, *Herr Kapitän*. Completely. A destroyer is also on its side. The *Alderhorst*. And we have also lost E-48 and E-25. No survivors. E-62 says it is a disaster. The explosion destroyed many buildings on land too. And sir, they think General Delsingen's headquarters has been hit. They have not yet got in close enough to check everything, but it looks very bad, sir.'

Geissler and Fröhmann stared at each other in dismay.

Just then, a voice shouted at them. '*Geissler!*'

Mindenhof, accompanied by the SS men who had accosted the Norwegian girl, were coming towards them at a trot. Geissler slowly unbuttoned his holster.

Fröhmann noticed the action. 'What are you doing!' he whispered.

'Being prepared for anything.'

The sailor was still standing close, waiting uncertainly for orders.

'Forsch,' he said quietly to the sailor.

'Sir?'

'Go back to the boat. Tell the lieutenant

to get ready to leave. Issue personal arms to everyone, then send two men back to me . . . armed. Then he's to wait. Now go. Quickly.'

'Yes, *Herr Kapitän.*' The man hurried away.

Mindenhof and his men arrived just as Forsch clambered back aboard the E-boat.

'Well, Geissler,' Mindenhof began, face glowing with triumph. 'You have all had it now. You have lost the Reich its prized ship. Shooting will be too good for you!'

'We know what has happened, Colonel,' Fröhmann said. 'We're on our way back to see what can be done.'

Mindenhof gave an ugly laugh. *'Done?* What's to be done? *The incompetent Kriegsmarine has cost the Führer his ship!* What's to be done except shoot the whole lot of you? And as for you, Geissler. How dare you obstruct my men in their duty? You have let a terrorist escape!'

The SS second lieutenant was looking eager for revenge. He stood to one side, eyes malevolently fixed on Geissler.

'What terrorist?'

'Do you think I am a fool?' Mindenhof snarled. 'We have been watching her! These men did not know it, but they had taken the correct action and were about to bring her in as a matter of course. I have information that suggests she is one of Ålvik's gang! Do you realize what you have done, Colonel?'

'Don't be ridiculous. Ålvik's gang are finished. My own team have destroyed many . . .'

'*You are coming with me!*'

'Have you finally gone mad? Are you arresting me, Mindenhof?'

'You have no power now, Geissler. From the message we have just received, it is quite clear that your general is dead. He is not around to protect you any more!'

'I would be very careful,' Fröhmann said to Mindenhof. 'Even you cannot dare . . .'

'You can go where the hell you please, Commander!' Mindenhof again snarled. 'All you naval people will have to answer to the Führer. But Geissler stays with me.'

The starting of the E-boat engines made them all look. Geissler took the opportunity to draw his pistol and point it at Mindenhof. The SS man's eyes widened in disbelief.

'Now *you* are the one who is mad. My men will cut you down.'

'But you will be dead.'

Two of Fröhmann's crew, sub-machine-guns ready, approached quickly. One was Forsch.

The SS men unslung their own weapons.

'Trouble, sir!' Forsch said as he drew up. His eyes were on the SS men.

'I don't think so,' Fröhmann replied quietly. 'Colonel Geissler is coming with me,' he added to Mindenhof. 'Will there be trouble?'

The cold eyes regarded Fröhmann with such hatred, it was as if they were trying to burn through him.

Mindenhof continued to glare, but said nothing.

Something suddenly buzzed past, to thump Mindenhof squarely in the chest. He staggered back, cap flying off the blond head, mouth opening wide. Blood poured out.

'What . . . ?' Geissler began.

The SS men froze for a fraction of a second, then began to look at the E-boat.

But the shot had not come from there. A report sounded faintly.

'*Sniper!*' Geissler bawled. '*Move, move!*'

They all dispersed, including the SS men. They left their colonel to die alone on the waterfront as they rushed for cover.

'Let's go!' Fröhmann said to Geissler. 'The boat. No point your staying here.'

'You don't have to say it twice.'

They hurried after the crewmen, making for

the waiting E-boat. The SS men did not fire at them.

From the top of a building far enough from the waterfront to allow a certain degree of security, Inge said to Skjel, 'Did you get him?'

'Of course.' Skjel was looking through the scope.

'And the Wehrmacht officer?'

'Making for the boat with his friend.'

'Don't kill him. I'm returning a favour.'

'If you say so,' Skjel said reluctantly. 'They're all Germans. So who cares if they kill each other?'

'He saved me from the SS. Leave him.'

'And the others?'

'We should get away from here. We've already stayed too long. The SS are going to go mad.'

'All right,' Skjel agreed, discretion winning.

Mölner had detached a flight of five aircraft – including his own – from an attack on a wave of Lancasters, when he'd been relayed the desperate call from Delsingen.

Now heading at altitude for Sognefjord, he was astonished to see the sky filled with Mosquitoes, all heading in his direction.

'*Break! Break!*' he called to his four Fw-190s.

*   *   *

'Oh look!' Bede said to Koos. 'Lots of trade.'

'Go for it, Blue Two!' he heard from Kearns.

Bede flung the Mosquito on to its back and latched on to the nearest Focke-Wulf.

The pilot spotted him and rolled away, but Bede hung on, going down after his prey.

The 190 began to head for altitude once more, but Bede had caught the incipient raising of the enemy aircraft's nose and had broken early out of his dive, to counter. As a result, when the 190 was pointing skywards again, Bede was waiting and had regained level flight as it flew right past the Mosquito's nose, going up. For the barest flash of time, the 190 was pinned directly before the guns of the Mosquito. If Bede were even infinitesimally slow to squeeze the trigger, the moment would be gone.

Bede was not slow.

The eight guns of the Mosquito raked the 190 from nose to tail. The aircraft simply disintegrated. No one got out.

'Yes, yes, *yes*!' Koos cried. 'You have him!'

'That was just breakfast, Rens. Let's look for lunch.'

Bede could not know that he had just killed Mölner.

*   *   *

The fifteen Mosquitoes that had survived the raid on the *Graf von Hiller* – despite the fact that some had suffered flak damage – fell upon the remaining four 190s. In a very short space of time the overwhelming odds took their toll and the four Focke-Wulfs fell terminally to earth. No Mosquitoes were lost during the one-sided battle.

Bede did not get his lunch, but shared a second kill with Kearns. Their job finished, the fifteen Mosquitoes headed for 35,000 feet, and home.

Kearns looked about him. Mosquitoes everywhere.

It was, he thought, a lovely sight.

In Berlin, Trudi Deger entered *Obergruppenführer* Honnenhausen's office. Overhead, the ominous drone of heavy bombers sounded. In the distance, the crump of bombs could be heard.

'Ah, Trudi,' he said. 'Another visit tonight from our friends. More news for me?'

Trudi seemed preoccupied. 'I wanted to come to you earlier, sir. But it has been very hectic.'

'I understand. There is much to do. And you do it well.'

'Thank you, sir.' She paused. 'It is a terrible thing that happened today. The *Graf von Hiller*. Lost!'

'Yes,' he said heavily. 'And I have lost a close friend too.'

'The general. I am so sorry.'

'It is war.'

She paused again, looking at him closely. In the dim lighting of the room, her face had taken on a beautiful, haunted quality.

'Who are you, sir?' she enquired softly.

Honnenhausen stared at her. 'What did you say?'

'I asked, who are you?'

'Is this a joke of some kind? Who am I? *Obergruppenführer* Honnenhausen, that's who! Are you suffering from concussion? That bomb that came close earlier . . .'

'I am perfectly all right. I know you are high in the Party . . . but who are you, really?'

'There has to be a reason for this nonsense, Trudi. I allow you great leeway, but you are putting yourself at great risk talking to me like that.'

'No I'm not. In the first place, if you were going to do anything, you would have done

so already. You would have called one of the
guards to drag me out.'

'And in the second?'

'It is not your way.'

'You know me so well?'

'I . . . would like to. Please. No, wait. Hear
what I have to say. Remember I brought you
that file on the Jews near Stolpe?'

'Yes.'

'You said you would attend to it.'

'Yes.'

'I went out there recently. They were still
there.'

'What did you do?'

'Nothing. I have not reported it. I have
checked other cases. Many other names that
I passed to you have not appeared on the
camp lists.'

'And have you reported those?'

'Of course not!' She sounded as if the very
idea should not even have occurred to him.

Honnenhausen looked at her like a dangerous
animal about to strike. 'Why?'

'Because I love you. You have always known
it. Now I have incriminated myself because of
it. At least, let me know the person who has
my love.'

'A patriot,' he said.

Whitehall, London

The two men looked at the report and felt pleased with themselves. The Mosquitoes had done the job. The supership was no more. Many strands had come together to produce that success. Not the least was the source of that first piece of information.

'I wonder if he misses Devon,' one of the men said to the other.

'Bound to. He has been out there since before the war, after all.'

'Think he's gone native?'

'He gave us that ship, didn't he? That's not the act of a man who's gone "native", as you put it. Major feather in his cap when the time comes for rewards for services to the Crown, above and beyond.'

'Brave man, doing what he does. Dangerous, dangerous job. Too bad he won't get a gong when this is all over. Not publicly anyway. Deserves the VC.'

'Well, he certainly can't be publicly recognized. Not for years. There'd be a lot of people out for revenge if they ever discovered who's been hiding in their midst.'

'Indeed. They also serve who . . .'

'Quite so, quite so.'

The men went back to dealing with matters

concerning people in delicate and dangerous situations.

Days later, having safely made her way with Olav Skjel out of Bergen, Inge Jarl was talking with one of the senior men in the resistance.

'You have done a good job,' he told her.

'I don't want to do that again,' she said. 'I nearly got myself caught.'

'You won't have to. Your report has added to the picture we're building.'

'But I only told you about things I saw – like the behaviour of the Germans to each other. Nothing very important.'

'But that's where you are wrong. Everything is important, especially morale. Their morale is very low after what has happened to their ship. Did you know Per was on that raid?'

'*Per?*' Her eyes shone. Then a fear came into them. 'Is he . . . all right?'

'Don't worry. Your Per is safe.'

'Oh thank God!'

'You still won't see him for a while.'

'I can wait, now that I know.'

'We heard from the Norwegian network in England. Apart from that battleship they sunk, they also destroyed many German guns, E-boats, and even seriously damaged a destroyer.

There's a lot of damage to much of the German *matériel* and supplies. It is a very serious blow. Two aircraft were lost. Such brave men.

'As for your little trip to Bergen, it will all help when the time comes. And killing that SS officer was also a good blow. The worse their morale, the better for us. Although I must say, it sounds strange to me about that Wehrmacht colonel. Perhaps he risked himself like that because you reminded him of his sweetheart.'

'Perhaps,' she said thoughtfully.

'But don't make a habit of saving German lives. Most of them are not like him. What would you do if you saw him again?'

'Probably kill him.'

1945

Inge did see her beloved Per again. He arrived in style after the German surrender, landing his Mosquito, now bearing Norwegian national markings, on an airfield that once again belonged to Norwegians.

Jo-Jo Kearns and Bede both survived. Kearns decided he would return to Australia to face his family. He was proud of his achievement and if they didn't like it, tough.

Wing Commander Smythe didn't. He went

on one mission too many when he shouldn't have. Returning in a badly shot-up aircraft piloted by Brack, it crashed on landing, killing them both.

Geissler also survived the war, but Fröhmann did not.

Out of uniform now, Geissler spent months after the end of the war searching the ruined Germany for the woman he considered he had so cowardly betrayed. The months turned into a year. Two years. The terrible truth about the camps gave him nightmares; but still he persisted with his search.

A third year came and went.

Then one day, he was sitting outside a coffee shop that they had once frequented before the horrors had descended on Germany. There was a British military post near the indifferently patched-up building.

'I wondered if you would come here,' a voice said. 'If you had survived.'

He could not believe his ears. He dared not look up, afraid of what he might see. Then he made himself do so.

He got to his feet slowly in wonder. She was as beautiful as he remembered, and did not look as if she had been in the camps at all. She looked as if she was not sure whether she should smile at him.

'I hear you have been turning Germany upside down looking for me,' she said. 'The British have a dossier on you. They think you are crazy.'

'I am ... I mean ... I mean I have been going crazy worrying about you all these years. I was such a coward. I cannot believe how cowardly.'

'You have the Iron Cross, First Class. That was not won by a coward.'

'But what I did. Deserting you when I should have stuck by you. That is the act of a coward.'

Her eyes were filming over. 'Did you love me so much that you carried this with you all through the war?'

He could not take his eyes off her. They gazed at her with a great hunger that was years old. He was not sure he could bear never to see her again.

'I have *never* stopped loving you. I swore if I ever got out alive, I would spend the rest of my days looking for you. And if they had taken you to the camps, I would search until I discovered where. You are my life.'

'The British know so much about you. They even know that you saved a girl in Norway from the SS, at a time when it was very dangerous for a Wehrmacht officer to do so. They found a report by an SS officer called Mindenhof, accusing you of treachery. He actually wrote down that you should be executed for deliberately allowing a known terrorist to escape.'

Geissler was stunned to realize how close he had come to death that day, at the hands of Mindenhof.

'She reminded me of you,' he said simply. 'I was trying to atone, I suppose, in some small way.'

'Not small. You could have been killed, and I would never have seen you again.'

'You . . . wanted to see me again?'

'At first, I hated you. You broke my heart . . .'

'I broke mine. But how do you know so much . . . ?'

'I escaped. I got away to England, and became an interpreter. I work for a British unit checking on the SS. That's how I came to hear about you, and your mad search.'

'If there is someone else . . . I will understand perfectly. I only wanted to know . . .' He said this, knowing if she turned away from him now, he could go quietly away somewhere and die.

'There is no one else,' she said. 'I can love only you, Ernst. Can't you see that?'

'How can you still love me? Look at what Germany has done . . .'

'Germany has destroyed itself too. *We* must not destroy ourselves.'

Geissler felt the years of hidden tears spring to his eyes.

She reached out to wipe them away gently.

Obergruppenführer Max Honnenhausen survived and made it to Australia with Trudi Deger. They married.

They have a different name and still live there comfortably. They have two children, and are now grandparents.

Max Honnenhausen, who was not born to that name, never made it back to his beloved Devon.

He got his Victoria Cross; but only Trudi knows of it.